KILKENNY COUNTY LIBRARY

Class. No. .... Acc No. ....

DATE OF RETURN	DATE OF RETURN	DATE OF RETURN

A SAINTLY KILLING

A FAITH MORGAN MYSTERY

MARTHA OCKLEY

WITH SPECIAL THANKS TO THEA BENNETT

LION FICTION

Published by Lion Fiction
an imprint of
Lion Hudson plc
Wilkinson House, Jordan Hill Road
Oxford OX2 8DR, England
www.lionhudson.com/fiction

ISBN 978 1 78264 091 2
e-ISBN 978 1 78264 092 9

First edition 2014

A catalogue record for this book is available from the British Library

Martha Ockley's
Faith Morgan Mysteries:

The Reluctant Detective
The Advent of Murder
A Saintly Killing

CHAPTER

1

Tuesday morning, 10:30 a.m. The calm before the storm.

Faith Morgan swept a scatter of confetti across the stone floor of the church porch and chivvied it towards the pile of dust and other detritus she was collecting by the door. Outside in the churchyard, the heat of the July sun was already intense. If only this glorious weather could hold out until the weekend! St James's Church, Little Worthy, was celebrating its 900th year on the Sunday coming. Faith's time as custodian, just twelve months so far, seemed an almost insignificant chapter in such a long history.

Despite the tranquillity of the old church's cool interior, she could feel her brain slipping into overdrive. *Commemorative services throughout the day. Lunchtime picnic for local families. Evening concert at the church by Christian rock group.*

And these were just the highlights of Sunday's very full agenda. Faith's usual A4 'to-do' sheet had swelled into a clipboard, bulging with lists and peppered with Post-it notes shouting "URGENT!"

She shook the last of the brightly coloured paper fragments from the broom. This morning, she'd promised herself a few moments of quiet time in the building that had become such an integral part of her life. The clipboard could wait. She'd tackle it with much more clarity and gusto after some calm meditation. She stood by the open door and closed her eyes, murmuring some words from the 26th Psalm. *O Lord, I love the habitation of your house and the place where your glory dwells.* The stone flags of the porch were firm and smooth beneath her feet. Birds twittered in the churchyard trees and from the village green came the distant hum of a car. The only slightly jarring note was the buzz of a chainsaw, across the fields at Shoesmith's Farm, where its new owner, none other than Jeremy Taylor, treasurer of the parish council, was carrying out extensive refurbishments to the farmhouse. But even that irritation was fading away, as the ancient peace of St James's possessed her...

"Morning, vicar!"

Faith started. A portly man with his sleeves rolled up was trundling a wheelbarrow past the door. Fred Partridge, one of the churchwardens. His red waistcoat was unbuttoned today – possibly a first.

Fred lowered the barrow and pulled a handkerchief out of his pocket to wipe the sweat from his brow.

"Sweeping up again?" He smiled at Faith. "Beyond the call of duty, I'd say."

"I enjoy it!" Faith replied.

It was always good to chat to Fred. His unassuming approach to life was very relaxing to be around, and from her earliest days as the first female incumbent of St James's, Faith had sensed that Fred was on her side, despite the fact that he was old enough to be her father, and might well have been expected to be a stickler for tradition. A couple of weeks ago, he'd shared with her the news that he'd been diagnosed with Type 2 diabetes. Faith had experienced some anxious moments over this, but Fred accepted the condition with equanimity. He assured her he was taking care with his diet, and following all the advice he'd been given. Apart from that, he intended to carry on as normal.

"Seen young Daniel about?" Fred asked. "He said he'd come by today, and give me a hand with the digging."

Faith shook her head. "I haven't. Not this morning."

Daniel Wythenshaw was a big-boned young man who lived with his parents on the other side of Little Worthy, about a mile and a half from St James's. His severe learning difficulties made it practically impossible for him to hold down a regular job, but he was devoted to Fred, and would work by his side for hours at a time.

"I'll keep an eye out for him," said Faith. "He's probably on his way."

Daniel was a friendly soul, and easily distracted. He might have encountered a walker with a dog, and stopped to chat.

"Right you are." Fred grasped the handles of the barrow and set off, heading for the new commemorative garden he was creating beside the vicarage. The highlight of the garden was to be a quiet, shady arbour where villagers could go to sit and reflect. Fred was a slow but thorough worker, and he was still at the hard-landscaping stage. The young trees to form the arbour hadn't arrived yet. It would be quite a task to get them all in the ground by Sunday.

Faith leaned on her broom handle. What she had said to Fred was true. She did enjoy cleaning the church. There was a rota for this, which none of the churchgoers would've expected their vicar to sign up to. But sweeping and dusting the ancient stones of St James's gave her a feeling of connection with past generations who had loved the place. Not just the previous incumbents – all men, of course – but the many women of Little Worthy, whose labours in caring for their church had gone unsung through the ages.

Faith shook herself out of her daydream. A grey-haired woman in a navy-blue dress and a white cardigan was bustling through the wicket gate. Pat Montesque, Fred's fellow-churchwarden. She looked as if she was on a mission.

What have I forgotten? Faith thought. *Oh, the bell ropes!* A key item on one of her lists was to contact Alfie Tarrent, a local builder, and ask him to hang a new set of bell ropes at St James's. The new ropes had been delivered, but fixing them at the top of the belfry was a specialist operation. She should really have rung Alfie yesterday.

Pat was hurrying up the path now, her face red. Faith's mobile jumped in her pocket. A text message. She sneaked a quick look at it in case it was something urgent:*still on for tonight? pls tell me u haven't forgotten.*

The message glowed accusingly. Faith's sister, Ruth, had organized a family meeting this evening to talk about their mother, and it wasn't a conversation Faith looked forward to. The memory lapses had been getting worse for months and, according to Ruth, the subject could not be avoided any longer.

Faith keyed in a quick reply to Ruth – *I'll be there!*

"Phew!" Pat hurried into the shade of the porch with a sigh of relief. "This heat is too much. Gracious me, what's all this?"

Pat hadn't noticed Faith's pile of sweepings, and she'd just kicked them all over the flagstones of the porch. She shook confetti from her white court shoe. "So sorry, dear. I didn't realize you were cleaning up."

"Don't worry about it," said Faith. She'd soon sweep up again. "Did you want to see me for something?"

"The anniversary booklet. We must get it to the p*rrr*inters!" Pat said. Little Worthy's longest-serving churchwarden was born and raised in Morningside. When she was particularly wound up about something, the strong Scottish "r" would often surface in her speech. "Our cont*rrr*ibutors are proving very tardy. I'm missing half the material!"

Faith winced, inwardly. The booklet was a collection of photographs and memoirs, and she was supposed to be writing the foreword for it. One more Post-it note that didn't shout loud enough…

"Pat, I'm so sorry. My piece is coming along. I'd just like to add a few final touches…"

In fact, she'd committed only a first draft to paper, and felt it hopelessly ill-fitted to the importance of the occasion.

"Of course I'm not referring to *you*, vicar. I've every confidence in *you*. It's the photographs of historic Little Worthy I'm concerned about. And as for that Hinkley woman… well!"

Pat pulled her spectacles off and rubbed the lenses vigorously with her handkerchief, a gesture that somehow managed to convey her deep distaste for the person she had just mentioned.

Faith sighed. She'd hoped they wouldn't return to this particular topic. Sal Hinkley had been commissioned to paint an image of St James's Church for the back cover of the booklet. The artist had trained at Winchester Art School more than thirty years ago, and had recently returned to the area after a long sojourn in the country of her birth, Australia. She was well known in the art world for her striking and sometimes controversial works, which sold for high prices.

"Pat," Faith said, "Sal was chosen to do the back cover by a democratic vote of our parishioners."

Pat made a noise that might have been a snort, and suggested that she thought democracy in church matters something of a novelty. "Artists are notoriously unreliable," she said. "I suspected from the outset that she'd miss the deadline."

"Sal will deliver on time," Faith said, with a tone that belied her lack of certainty. "I'm sure she just wants the painting to be perfect."

Pat sighed. "It's a t*rrr*avesty that our own dear Gwen was passed over for this commission."

Faith struggled not to roll her eyes. Hinkley-gate, as her mother had mischievously called it, would not rest. Local artist Gwen Summerly, who just happened to be a close friend of Pat, was renting a house just off the village green, having been born and bred in Little Worthy and its environs. The only thing she and Sal Hinkley had in common was that they had attended the art school at the same time. Gwen now taught art classes on an informal basis and her speciality was watercolour paintings of local scenes, most notably the glorious cottage gardens that abounded in the village.

"Gwen's one of us," Pat continued, as if that crucial argument should settle the dispute once and for all.

Faith took a deep breath. She really must say something. Pat was a good-hearted woman. It was a shame that she occasionally lapsed into intolerance.

"Sometimes an outsider may see with a clearer vision," Faith said.

"I'm *rrr*eally not at all sure what you mean by *that...*"

Faith was spared from having to explain herself by the sight of two people walking up the path. A broad-shouldered man with a slight stoop and a matting of gingery stubble on his cheeks, and beside him, holding his arm, a trim woman with her hair styled in a sleek bob. Percy Cartwright, the last of Little Worthy's dynasty of blacksmiths, and his wife, Andrea. As they stepped into the porch, Percy pulled off his tweed cap, revealing a shock of white hair.

"Good morning! Warm one, isn't it?" Andrea said. She held out an envelope. "Here's our photograph, at last. Sorry for the delay, Pat."

Pat thanked her. She opened the envelope and pulled out the contents.

"Ah, look at this, Faith. Those were the days. Not a car to be seen." She held out an old black-and-white photograph.

Despite the lack of motor vehicles, Little Worthy was clearly recognizable in the photo. A young boy was leading two Shire horses across the Green towards the forge, where a man in a leather apron stood with his arms folded.

"Is that your grandfather, Percy?" Faith asked. "He looks like you."

Percy twisted his cap in his large, knotted fingers. "My great-grandfather," he said.

"So sad that you are selling up," Pat said. "The village won't be the same without the forge."

The Cartwrights had sold the old forge building to Free Foods, a chain of organic outlets that owned a farm shop in a village a few miles from Little Worthy. They were looking to expand, and planned to knock down the forge and build a spanking new health food emporium on the site. For many years Percy had made wrought-iron garden ornaments at the forge, but he was retiring now. He and Andrea were moving to France to run a hostel off the pilgrim's trail, near to Lourdes.

"When do you leave?" Faith asked.

Percy was silent, looking down at his boots. Faith didn't know the man well – he wasn't a churchgoer – but he always struck her as something of a lost soul. It was hard to read the expression in his face now, but it must be an emotional time for him. Several generations of Cartwrights had worked at the forge. Yet even if Percy stayed on in Little Worthy, he would be the last of the line. Faith knew that Andrea was his second wife. The first had passed away not long after their only son died in a car accident.

Andrea slipped a hand through her husband's arm. "Next weekend. We can't wait."

Andrea was a Catholic, and had been a teacher at the local Catholic school. It was generally acknowledged by the inhabitants of Little Worthy that without the love and the warm, supportive energy of Andrea, Percy might have fallen into serious depression.

"I'm sure it will be very rewarding," Faith said. "And you, Percy – are you looking forward to the change?"

"It will be good." The old man's eyes, faded from so many years of working with fire and hot metal, had a distant look. Faith wished that she'd got to know him better. He had given up attending services at St James's after the loss of Rory, so he had never been part of her congregation, even though his wife and son were buried in the churchyard.

The couple said their goodbyes and walked off, arm in arm.

"Thanks for the wonderful photo," Faith called after them. She turned to Pat. "What good people. They'll be greatly missed in the village."

Pat leaned close and whispered: "My friend Barbara – you know? From the WI? *She'll* be very glad to see the back of them."

"Why?" Faith couldn't picture the Cartwrights as anything other than exemplary members of the community.

"The smoke from the forge!" Pat continued, her lips pursed. "Barbara lives right next door and she said it smelled dreadful. Just this morning her washing was *rrruined*!"

Faith suppressed a smile. The speed that gossip could spread through Little Worthy was quite fascinating.

Pat clearly had plenty more to say about Barbara's spoiled sheets, but she was interrupted by heavy footsteps, thudding along the side of the church. Fred came staggering into the porch, his face horribly pale. "C-call – an ambulance," he gasped. His soil-smeared hands were shaking. Faith thought for a horrible moment that he was having a heart attack.

"Fred?" She ran to his side. "Fred, what is it?"

"Sal Hinkley!" said Fred. "She's in the hut. I... I saw her on the floor!"

"Is she ill? What's wrong?"

Fred struggled for breath. "I think she's... dead."

Faith heard Pat suck in a breath. Her own senses sharped as adrenaline kicked in.

"Steady, Fred. Take some slow, deep breaths. Well done for coming so quickly. Pat – can you dial 999? Ask them to send an ambulance, right away? Tell them a woman's been taken ill. No details yet, but it's a possible fatality."

"Of course." Pat hurried away to the telephone in the vestry.

"Let's go," Faith said, laying a hand on Fred's arm. It seemed to calm him a little. His breath slowed and his colour began to return. "Show me, Fred."

The quickest way to the dilapidated hut that Sal Hinkley was using as a studio was through the side gate of the churchyard and over a rickety fence onto the rough pastureland that bordered the church. Fred headed that way, stumbling as he hurried between the gravestones.

Faith followed, her heart banging against her ribs. She could just catch the words that Fred was muttering to himself: "I took my thermos… I wanted to ask if she'd like a cuppa. I never thought… Oh dear. Oh dear, dear me…"

She caught up as he clambered over the fence. "Fred. The hut. Did you go inside?"

Fred's eyes widened at her sharp tone. She could have bitten back the words, seeing the awkward, embarrassed expression on his gentle face. It wasn't the way to speak to a parishioner and friend. It was several years now since she had left to follow her vocation, yet the old behaviour still kicked in as soon as she was confronted with an emergency.

"Y… yes," Fred said.

Faith couldn't stop herself asking, but she spoke softly this time. "Did you touch anything?"

Fred nodded. "Only Sal," he said, "I wanted to see if she was… all right."

They were at the hut now.

"Wait here." Faith pushed open the peeling wooden door, using her elbow so that she would leave no fingerprints.

It was very hot inside the hut, and there was a strong smell of turpentine. Sal Hinkley lay on the floor beside her easel. She was wearing a long dress of green linen and her slight body looked almost graceful, with arms uplifted and her head turned to one side. Faith was struck by the dramatic mane of grey-streaked red hair that flared around the painter's heart-shaped face.

There were several dark, bluish-red marks on Sal's slim neck. Faith stared at them, and for an odd moment she thought they might be paint. But the painting on the easel, the view of St James's Church, was a different palate entirely.

As Faith knelt to feel for a pulse she knew would not be there, she realized that the marks were bruises.

Sal Hinkley had been strangled.

CHAPTER

2

The midday sun beat down on the roofs of three police vehicles, one of them an unmarked van which housed a forensics team. They were parked up in a line on the dry grass of the paddock. The hut had been taped off, and the investigating officers were inside. Faith stood watching with a group of onlookers, knowing she must stay with her parishioners, despite the vestigial urge to climb under and run to join the team at the crime scene.

"This is just so awful." Pat dabbed at her eyes with a pristine pocket-handkerchief. "Whatever one might think of Ms Hinkley's lifestyle, one would never have wished something like this upon her."

Faith turned to comfort her, but Jeremy Taylor, who'd come running over the fields from Shoesmith's Farm as soon as he heard the police sirens, beat her to it.

"Now then, Pat," he said, putting an arm around the churchwarden's shoulders.

Pat rallied a little and tucked her handkerchief in the pocket of her cardigan. "But how did she die? Why should such a thing happen?" she asked.

Fred, standing a little apart from the group, shook his head sadly. The discovery of Sal Hinkley's body had sent him into himself. He had become even quieter than usual.

"We must leave such speculation to the experts," Jeremy nodded in the direction of the police vehicles. His thin face was flushed and his sharp nose had caught a little too much sun. "I think perhaps some hot, sweet tea is in order. I'd invite you all to the farmhouse, but the builders, you know... such a mess..."

"Poor Jeremy," Pat said. "So distressing for you. Another death on the property. And so soon after Trevor... It almost seems there's something – malevolent – about the place."

Faith caught the frown on Jeremy's face, even if Pat didn't. He'd bought Trevor Shoesmith's ramshackle farm after the farmer's suicide, last year. He was in the process of completely revamping the buildings, eradicating the chaos and dilapidation that Trevor had inhabited.

"Mrs Montesque! You're letting your imagination run away with you." George Casey, the press officer for the diocese, had driven over from Winchester as soon as he heard about Sal's death. His close-cropped head with its receding hairline jutted forward as he spoke: "As you say, Ms Hinkley led a somewhat unconventional life, which no doubt will provide an explanation for this sad occurrence. We mustn't dwell on the events of the past. Jeremy is doing an incredible job at the farmhouse. If it weren't for the building works I'm sure he'd be delighted to give us a tour and provide us with some tea..."

George gave Faith a meaningful look, implying that it was her duty to step in and offer refreshments at the church. She was just thinking that perhaps she should comply, when one of the police team – a tall man with dark hair – came out from the hut.

"Hello, Faith!" Detective Inspector Ben Shorter ducked his frame beneath the tape and came towards them. "We can't go on meeting like this."

Faith sensed a frisson of disapproval from Pat and George, and cursed Ben inwardly. Did he really have to seem like he was *enjoying* it? Her employers and parishioners all knew about her previous career with the force, of course, but it naturally didn't always sit comfortably with them. Especially when Ben was behaving in such a familiar way. He had no reason to. It was a good four months since they'd even spoken to each other, and that had been purely professional. Years had passed since they were anything more than acquaintances. Faith was suddenly aware that she was sweating. A hand plucked at Faith's arm. George Casey.

"This incident is not a church matter," he muttered. "Please keep your distance, Faith. We don't want any adverse publicity. Not with the anniversary upon us."

George's attempts to distance the church seemed risible in the circumstances, and she saw the look of bemused incredulity plain on Ben's face. His gaze passed quickly from George to her.

"Forensics are doing their thing," he said, with a slight dismissive curl of his lip. 'But no time of death yet. I understand that you knew the victim?"

Faith took a deep breath, steadied herself. The first few moments of any encounter with Ben were never easy.

"A little. She's been working on a commission for the St James's commemorative booklet."

Someone else was coming out of the hut. A slim woman in the hooded white bodysuit of the forensics team. Faith stared.

There was something familiar about the woman's stride.

Ben flicked a glance over his shoulder.

"Harriet. What have you got for me?"

Faith swallowed. Of course. Harriet Sims, head pathologist with the Hampshire constabulary. Faith had met her last December at a disastrous dinner party, when Ben had materialized with the leggy, red-haired woman in tow. Her stomach tightened at the memory.

"The heat is complicating things." Harriet tucked a lock of that vivid hair under the edge of her hood. Her voice sounded thin and apologetic. "The body's probably been there overnight. That's all I can give you at the moment."

Ben's mouth tightened. "Not enough. I need something more precise."

"That's all I can give you at the moment," Harriet repeated, coldly.

Faith couldn't help a rush of gratification as she watched Harriet walk slowly back to the hut. Clearly things were not going too well between her and Ben – if they were going at all. Faith gave herself a mental shake. Such thoughts were not in any way charitable.

She turned her thoughts back to Sal, and a sudden memory surfaced. Faith glimpsed her yesterday evening, just for an instant. It had slipped her mind until now.

"I saw Sal. Yesterday. At seven o'clock," she said.

Ben's eyes flicked to her face, clear and intense as the summer sky above.

"How can you be sure of the time?"

"I was at the church, locking up the main door before I went home. I heard the clock chime the hour. I turned to leave and I saw her in the paddock, wearing that green dress."

"Did she speak to you?"

"No. She was quite a long way away. I think she may have seen me; she looked round. But she didn't wave."

"That's odd."

"Not really." To be honest, Sal had never seemed particularly friendly. Cold, even. "Sal kept herself to herself," she said.

"What was she doing in the paddock at that time?" Ben's eyes were needling Faith. She had to look away.

"I assumed she was going to paint at the hut for a couple of hours. The evenings are so light at this time of year."

"Anyone with her?"

"No." Faith said, feeling her face grow even hotter. Surely it was clear from what she had said that Sal was alone. She would have mentioned, immediately, if there had been anyone accompanying the artist. Ben should know that.

"Did you see her enter the hut?"

"You can't see the hut from the church. Just a small area of the paddock." Faith couldn't help a slight briskness creeping into her voice.

"Right." Ben flashed a smile at her. He always knew when he had got her riled, and questioning her like a civilian was sure-fire.

"Sal is – was – lodging with the Wythenshaws at River Lodge B&B," Faith continued. "It's about a mile and a half on the other side of Little Worthy." As she spoke, she thought about Daniel. Had he shown up after all?

"I'll send someone over," said Ben. "Any next of kin?"

Faith pulled out her mobile, checking through the directory of numbers. "The only contact Sal gave us was her art dealer, Patrick Mills. I don't think she had other family."

"Call him," Ben said.

"Me?" asked Faith.

Ben shrugged. "You have a more personal touch."

Faith's temper flared. How could be so glib?

"We'll be in the church," Jeremy interrupted. "'Pat says we can brew up in the vestry. Would you care for a cup of tea, officer?"

"Tea? No," Ben said, his eyes narrowing. "And it's Detective Inspector."

Jeremy's flushed face turned a shade darker.

"You'd all better remain here, for the time being," Ben added. "We'll need to ask you some questions.'"

Jeremy's chin went up, but he kept quiet. He, Pat and George set off over the rough ground towards the churchyard, Fred following slowly behind them. Faith dialled the number for Patrick Mills's gallery in London. The man himself picked up on the first ring, enunciating his name in a precise, aristocratic voice.

"What's that?" he stammered, as Faith gave him the awful news. "Sal? But she's got an exhibition coming up! Her first one-woman show in this country for decades! It'll be a sell-out."

"It's very sad that she won't be there to enjoy it," Faith said.

Patrick spluttered on. He seemed to be having some difficulty coming to terms with the news.

"I just can't get my head round this," he was saying. "Sal was so vibrant. Full of life force. I can't take it in. Was she unwell? What happened?"

"We don't know," Faith said, carefully. "The circumstances are a little suspicious. The police are here."

There was a short silence at the other end. Then Patrick said, in a more businesslike tone: "Poor Sal. Dreadful. Naturally

I'll take care of the funeral arrangements. No expense spared. The commission on the sales from the exhibition will cover it."

Faith was taken aback. Both by the generosity of the offer, but also the crude mention of profit at such a sombre time. "Thank you," she managed.

Another silence, and then Patrick said, "What about that ex-husband of hers?"

"I'm sorry?"

"McGarran. David McGarran. The fellow she left all those years ago."

Faith was confused. She'd known Sal's status as a divorcee – it was just another black mark in the catalogue that had made her the "wrong choice" in Pat's book. But she knew nothing more about the man, and this was the first time she'd heard his name.

"Is he local?" she asked.

"Is who local?" Ben appeared beside her in his short-sleeved police shirt, his brown forearms lean and strong. She caught the warm, citrus tang of his aftershave.

Mills told her that McGarran ran a picture-framing shop in Winchester, so Sal had said. "Should be easy to find him."

"Thank you for that," Faith said to the art dealer. "I had no idea."

Faith pocketed her phone and explained the gist of the call to Ben.

"Well, well," he said, smiling. "A bitter ex."

He pressed a button on his radio. It crackled into life, and a familiar voice uttered a call sign. Sergeant Peter Gray, Ben's usual sidekick, and a member of Faith's congregation. Peter, the host of that memorable dinner party last year, where Ben had turned up with Harriet.

"Peter?" Ben's voice was gruff and matter of fact. "We've identified a suspect in Winchester. I'm heading there now."

We. Ben had spoken as if Faith was still a police officer. Still one of the team.

"Hold on," said Faith. "David McGarran is hardly a suspect!" She felt she had to say it, even though she knew what Ben's response would be.

He already had his car keys in his hand. "Isn't he? You know the statistics, Fay. Nine times out of ten in cases like this, the victim is related to the killer."

Fay. His pet name for her, back in the day. Back when they were together; a couple. It was meant to disarm her caution, but in this case it just made her sad.

"You were possibly the last person to see Sal Hinkley alive," he said. "Aside from whoever dropped by later and attacked her. I'll need your help. We'll speak soon." He turned away, hurrying to his car.

Faith made her way back over the fence and through the churchyard to St James's. Hopefully there would still be some tea in the pot. Her mouth felt very dry.

"Do you think we should postpone the celebrations on Sunday?" Faith asked. She was washing up the mugs in the vestry's small sink. George Casey stood at her side with a tea towel over his arm, looking distinctly uneasy with his role. Faith guessed his wife did the majority of the washing-up in the Casey household.

"No, no!" he said, his brow creasing in consternation. "Out of the question."

"I just thought…" Faith hesitated, swirling her hands in the sudsy water. "*A time to weep, and a time to laugh; a time to mourn, and a time to dance …*"

George nodded. "Ecclesiastes. Very fitting. But Ms Hinkley wasn't one of your congregation. She wasn't even one of us. One of our local people. We must keep the show on the road."

Faith wasn't sure, but George was right about one thing – Sal really had little connection to Little Worthy and the church. And it *would* be a shame to postpone the anniversary celebrations, so long in the planning. Most of the village were hoping to turn out. And yet...

Faith felt a sudden sorrow at the memory of Sal, last evening. Of the way that she paused, brushing her heavy hair aside and giving a quick half-glance towards the church before hurrying on across the paddock. What was she thinking about? Did she have any inkling of what was about to unfold? Or was her mind just full of colours and shapes as she planned out her next canvas? Faith pushed the sadness aside and rinsed the mugs, passing them to George one by one.

"All done," Peter Gray came through into the vestry, running his fingers over his short, sandy hair. "I've spoken to everyone. How's it going, Faith? You all right?"

Peter was so different from Ben. So open and engaging. If he felt cynicism, he concealed it well. There was no need for Faith to defend herself with him. He knew and appreciated both sides of her, the ex-police officer and the woman with a vocation. They could be – they *were* – good friends. But then, of course, they had never had a relationship.

"A bit shocked. We all are. Sal was – well, she was Sal," Faith said, picturing the artist's pale face and her tumbled hair as she lay on the floor of the hut. "Will you need to interview anyone again?"

"Not sure. Depends how things go. We'll check out the alibis, and see what comes up with the rest of the investigation."

"We've been advised that we may be contacted," George said, wielding the tea towel with a frown on his face. "Both Pat and Jeremy were rather upset, I'm afraid. All this is very distressing for them."

"Routine procedure," Peter said. "We may not need to speak to them again, but we can't rule it out at this stage." He winked at Faith. She gave a tiny shake of her head, reminding him that she was on the other side now, had different priorities. The care of her flock must come first. She didn't know Jeremy very well, but he seemed rather highly strung. The few times she'd seen him drive through the village in his Jaguar on his way to speak with builders and architects he'd given her a brisk wave. No doubt a police interview would be very onerous for him. Pat would rather enjoy the opportunity to hold forth, Faith suspected. But poor Fred would be very ill at ease.

"Off home to put your feet up, sergeant?" George Casey said, polishing the last of the mugs and lining it up with the others on the draining board. In contrast to the others, he seemed completely unruffled by his interrogation.

"No such luck. The kids will be going crazy for a game of footy," Peter smiled broadly. Chalk and cheese, he and Ben, Faith thought. Perhaps that was why they worked so well together.

"Oh, by the way." George nudged Faith's elbow. "Sal's commission. Did she… er… finish it?" His light eyes glowed.

"I think so," Faith replied, surprised by his eagerness. He'd never expressed any enthusiasm for Sal's work before.

"That painting of St James's?" Peter interrupted. "Been commandeered, I'm afraid, as evidence."

"Ah, of course." George smiled, and headed off out of the vestry.

"We need it back, Peter," Faith said. "We have to get it copied for our booklet."

Peter smiled at her and frowned at the same time. Faith could see he was torn. "We need to have it dusted for prints, but I'll see what I can do."

Faith followed him through the church and watched as he hurried back to the paddock and his vehicle. Back inside, Pat was nowhere to be seen – she must have headed home to recover from the ordeal of being questioned. Fred had disappeared, too. George Casey and Jeremy Taylor were sitting on one of the pews, talking earnestly with their heads close together. She was about to go over and check that Jeremy was all right, when a man in blue overalls strolled into the porch.

"West Forest Tree Nursery," he said. "Delivery for you."

"Ah, thank you," said Faith.

"Bad time, is it?" said the man, nodding at the police tape.

"You could say that."

By the time Faith had shown him where to park his lorry, and guided him and his sturdy sack-barrow back and forth to Fred's arbour (hoping that she remembered correctly where Fred was going to site all the different trees) it was past six o'clock. She was washing her hands in the vestry when her mobile buzzed.

Faith?????? Another text from Ruth.

A surge of panic. Faith checked her watch. She was due at her sister's house fifteen minutes ago.

Sorry, got held up. See you in 30. Faith responded, and jogged for the car. No time to drop in on Pat and Fred and check that they were OK. No time, either, to swing by the vicarage and freshen up. Ruth would just have to take her as she was – hot and sweaty.

As the car pulled out onto the Green, Faith's eye was caught by a movement in the window of one of the cottages. Gwen Summerly's. She thought she saw the painter's tall figure in the shadows. Faith had assumed she was out. Could Gwen really have been oblivious to all the police activity just 100 yards from her front door? The curtain dropped back into place and the figure vanished.

Gwen made no secret of her resentment of Sal's success. And Sal hadn't been exactly reticent in expressing her derision for Gwen's watercolours. But surely it was just a case of *professional* rivalry.

Faith pressed the accelerator and sped off through Little Worthy.

CHAPTER

3

The fields looked drab and brown under the intense sun as Faith drove through the countryside towards Winchester. There wasn't much in the way of summer grass this year. A group of hungry-looking cows stood by a gate with their heads down and their tails swishing against the flies. Maybe the farmer would bring them some hay later, Faith hoped.

As if on cue, her stomach rumbled. Lunch wasn't a high priority on her agenda at the best of times – and she'd managed to miss breakfast as well today. A hastily eaten banana at 7 a.m. didn't really count. She glanced at the clock. The bad news – over eleven hours since that banana. The good news – if she put her foot down, she might just make the Free Foods outlet in the next village before closing time. A treat for Ruth would go some way to making up for Faith's late arrival at the family conference.

The shop's manager, a young woman called Farrah Jordan, was pulling down the shutters as Faith drove up. Her pretty, olive-skinned face broke into a vivid smile.

"Hello, Faith! You're just in time. Another five minutes, and we'd have been gone."

Farrah had grown up in a mixed-heritage family on a council estate in London. She'd worked hard to build a career for herself – first as a *sous-chef* in a well-known London restaurant, and now as a leading light in the Free Foods organics business.

"I'm so sorry to turn up just as you're closing," Faith said as she eased herself out of the car. Her dress was damp with sweat all down the back. "I'm due at my sister's – and I'm so late. I need a peace offering. I was thinking maybe one of your wonderful carrot cakes?"

"How's our favourite vicar?" Farrah's husband, Jasper Jordan, the son of a local farmer, ducked under the shutter and held out his hand. His fair skin was flushed red with the heat. "We were just talking about what we're going to sell from our stall on Sunday. Cakes, of course – and all sorts of pastries. It's so hot, we thought we might do some gazpacho as well, in paper cups so it's easy for people to take away."

Farrah and Jasper were a hard-working young couple, always warm and welcoming to all their customers. Faith had been pleased to offer them the opportunity to run a stall at the anniversary celebrations. George Casey had tried to argue against this. *Free Foods is a commercial enterprise – is it really appropriate to include them in a church occasion?* Faith had stuck to her guns. It couldn't be very easy, selling quality, premium-priced produce in the current economic climate, but Farrah and Jasper were doing well. It felt good to help them out – and it would be great to have them around on the day. Everyone would enjoy their delicious cakes and healthy snacks. What could be the harm in that?

"Gazpacho sounds great," Faith said. "Actually, there's something I have to tell you. A piece of rather sad news."

"Oh, no." Jasper pushed the shutter back up and gestured for her to follow him into the shop. "Nothing personal, I hope?"

"No, no." Faith explained about Sal Hinkley's death.

"You're kidding!" Farrah's eyes were wide. "Sal? Wow."

"Yes. And – I'm afraid it looks as if there are some suspicious circumstances. The police are making an investigation."

Faith's voice sounded very loud in the empty shop. Her words had created a sudden silence. Farrah flashed an anxious glance at her husband. He shrugged and walked over to the counter where the cakes were kept. They both looked a little uncomfortable with the news.

"Is something wrong?" Faith asked as Jasper bent to lift out a cake, his shoulders tight and tense. And then she could have kicked herself. *Is something wrong?* Such questions were Ben's province. She was not here to interrogate this young couple, just because a moment's uncharacteristic behaviour made her uneasy. Those days were long gone.

"No, no," Jasper said, turning round. "Sal wasn't our favourite customer, I have to say. A very 'picky' lady. Always trying and then not buying. But we wouldn't have wished this on her. No way. Here you go, Faith. One large carrot cake. Shall I pop it in a box for you?"

"Perfect! What do I owe you?"

"Nothing!" Farrah said, smiling again now. "With our compliments, Faith. We're so happy that you asked us to run the stall for you."

Perhaps Faith had imagined it, that brief moment of tension. She tucked the cake box under the front seat of her little car and drove on along the dual carriageway around Winchester to the new-build estate where her sister lived.

Ruth's "doll's house", as Faith always thought of it – so picture-perfect with the miniature conifers in the front garden, and the pale blue, draped blinds at all the windows – was looking as fresh as ever, despite the heat. She pressed the bell, and held out the cake box, ready to drop it into straight into her sister's outstretched hands as the door opened.

"Hello, Faith. Long time no see."

Faith almost dropped the box on the step. Not Ruth, but a stocky, smiling man with fair hair fading to white confronted her in the narrow hallway.

"B-Brian!" Faith said.

It was a very long time since Faith had been in such close proximity with her sister's ex-husband – face to face, like this. Almost two decades, in fact. She'd seen him once or twice, at a distance, picking up Sean, his son, driving him away from Ruth's house for an evening or a weekend. They hadn't spoken, though. Brian had put on a little weight, but the same dimples were there as he smiled, just like the day he'd married Ruth.

Faith's throat tightened. *What right had he to smile at her, this man who had treated her sister with such callous disregard? The man who had thought nothing of leaving a pregnant young wife for a torrid affair with one of his work colleagues?*

"You're looking very respectable," Brian said, eyeing Faith's black cotton blouse. She'd removed the dog collar before getting out of the car. "I suppose you have to, these days. I was thinking about you, the other night. That musical – *My Fair Lady* – was on the telly. It reminded me of you, singing your heart out with the am-drams."

Faith found herself blushing. Same old Brian. In one of her summer breaks from university she'd been offered the role of Eliza Doolittle in a local production, but she doubted she could get into the wasp-waisted green dress with the bustle that she'd worn for the finale of the show now. Her hairstyle, too, had been much more extravagant than today's neat, functional shoulder-length bob. She'd had it permed for the show, and the mass of curls had been piled up on top of her head with just a few strands falling down at the sides. Altogether a very different Faith Morgan from the woman who stood outside Ruth's house right now. A very long time ago now, and a whole other world.

"I would have changed," she said, "but I rushed straight here."

"You were quite a corker, I thought. But of course I only had eyes for your lovely sister," Brian said. "Shall I take that for you?" He reached for the box.

"I brought it for Ruth," Faith said, holding on to it. What was he *doing* here?

She kept her eyes fixed on the cardboard lid of the box; unsure whether it was a good idea to let him see the expression of dislike and disapproval that must be showing on her face.

It was too much, this instant assumption that they were on friendly terms. And his comment about only having eyes for Ruth was out of order, given the callous way he had walked out on her, once his infatuation had cooled. Faith's gaze slipped from the cake box to the floor, and she saw, with a frisson of distaste, that her ex-brother-in-law was wearing what looked like a brand-new pair of sheepskin slippers. *Slippers?* Was he planning to stay the night?

"Ah, sorry – *of course* it's for Ruth," Brian said, his jokey tone losing some of its assurance. "No worries. If you want to give it to her, she's just through in the kitchen. Come on in, Faith. G&T? You look like you need one."

"Just tonic, thank you," said Faith.

Brian headed in the direction of the dining room and the drinks cabinet, as Ruth came running from the kitchen. She flung her arms around Faith – an unusually warm welcome.

"Sorry I'm late," Faith said, holding the cake box at an awkward angle to keep it out of the way of her sister's hug. "I brought you this. Carrot cake. But Roo – what, why..." She flicked a look towards the clink of glasses in the dining room.

Ruth gripped Faith's elbows with tense, eager fingers. Her eyes were very bright. "Oh, Faith. Don't be like that. We're taking things slowly, but...'

"Taking *what* slowly?" asked Faith.

"It's not working with Susie," whispered Ruth, her face aflame with joy. "She's been treating him so badly."

"Please tell me he hasn't moved in...?"

"It's only temporary," said Ruth. "But so far it's going really well."

Faith swallowed. She must choose her words carefully. It was so painful to see the same light in her sister's eyes that had been there on her wedding day. *I can't bear for her to be hurt again. It mustn't, mustn't be allowed to happen...*

"Roo – are you sure you're OK with this? With him living here?'

"I'm over the moon!' Ruth broke eye contact and glanced down at the box. "Oh, Faith, you've brought a cake. That's perfect."

So. This was more than just an informal family meeting about their mother's health, Faith realized with a sinking heart. This was a special occasion to officially notify her that Brian was back in residence.

But what about Sean, Ruth and Brian's son? Where might he fit in to all of this? Faith felt a sudden pang for her nephew. He was away at university, but it would surely be very disturbing for him, this unexpected intrusion into his home of the father who had living with another woman for twenty years – almost his entire life, in fact.

"Mind your toes!" Brian edged out of the dining room with a tray of glasses.

Faith backed away from him in the narrow hall, and made her way to the living room, where she sat down on the sofa. Ruth bustled with plates and forks for the cake and then came to sit beside her. Brian distributed the drinks and sat on a chair by the window. He looked a little put out. Clearly, he felt he should be the one sitting next to Ruth.

"You're such a star, turning up with this cake. It looks utterly yummy. As good as home-made," Ruth said, cutting three large slices.

Faith smiled. Free Foods could always be relied upon to come up with something excellent. Ruth leaned closer and laid a hand on her arm.

"I need to ask you a favour," she said. "You know Mum's got an appointment in West London on Thursday morning, for a second opinion on her diagnosis. She's coming to stay here the night before. I was going to take her, but—"

"Oh, Ruth, no," said Faith, cutting off her sister. "Don't ask me." She thought of the clipboard and all the Post-it notes. "The church anniversary is on Sunday. I'm up to my eyes in it."

Ruth's face fell. "Mum's booked to see a top dementia specialist," she said. "If she can't make it, we'll have to wait months to get another appointment. I really wanted to go – but

Peter went off sick yesterday. He'll be off all week. I absolutely can't leave work, not with the boss out of the picture."

Ruth was PA to the chief executive of the local council. His responsibilities were extensive, and Faith knew there was no way her sister could opt out of holding the fort in his absence.

Faith took a long breath. It was so rare to see Ruth so happy – albeit a somewhat precarious happiness, in Faith's opinion. It seemed uncharitable to dampen her spirits by refusing to help out. Her work would get done – it always did, somehow. It was not long since midsummer day, and the evenings were still long. She would just work on through – round the clock, if she had to.

"I'll do it," she said.

"Oh, Faith!" Ruth hugged her again. "Bless you!"

"Can I top you up, ladies?" Brian asked.

Faith had barely sipped her tonic, but Brian, she noticed, has finished his drink already. She shook her head.

He went out to the kitchen. He'd be gone for a few minutes at least. Faith took her sister's hand.

"Ruth, I have to ask this. Are you sure that you're doing the right thing, letting him move back in? What he did to you…"

Ruth whipped her hand away. "How can you ask that? What about your Christian principles, Faith? Forgiveness? Doesn't that figure somewhere for you?"

"Of course." Faith leaned back against the sofa cushions. "Forgiveness is crucial. But – only where's it's earned. He behaved so badly to you, Roo. Hurt you so much. He deserted you, left you – when you were so young – to bring up his child alone. If you want to talk about principles…"

"I don't," Ruth said, firmly. "And I find your attitude rather negative. I love him. He loves me and he's come back to me, and that's all that matters."

"And Sean? How does he feel about it?"

"We haven't told him yet," Ruth said, her voice low. She looked down at the immaculate cream-coloured carpet, clearly feeling uncomfortable.

Brain poked his head round the door. "Sorry, girls. Don't mean to interrupt the sisterly pow-wow – Roo, have we got any more lemons?"

Ruth stood up. "Did you check the back of the fridge?" she said. "I think there's a half one there." She left the room, not casting a look back.

Faith was left alone on the sofa. A feeling of isolation possessed her. She was the odd one out here, excluded from the intense aura that enclosed Ruth and Brian. But for how long would it last, this second honeymoon?

Much later, deeply asleep in her bedroom with the windows wide open to allow in as much cool air as possible, Faith was awoken by an uncanny screech. The luminous digits on her alarm clock told her it was 2 a.m. She lay very still, listening, but the eerie cry didn't come again. The bedroom door creaked and she started, grabbing instinctively for the duvet that wasn't there – it was folded up on a chair in the corner. The night was way too hot for covers.

"*Me-yow-ow!*"

A large tabby cat, his soft fur striped with black and silver, slinked around the half-open door and padded over to the bed.

"Beast!" Faith leaned to stroke his head. "Was that you making that awful noise? You scared me. What are you doing up here?"

The Beast, having been firmly ejected from the bedroom on several previous occasions (he wasn't Faith's cat, just an occasional visitor, so too much intimacy seemed a little inappropriate), normally slept downstairs in the kitchen.

He purred, arching his back against her hand.

"What's got into you?" Faith was just about to relax her usual rule and encourage him to jump up beside her when the cat sprinted across the room and hopped up onto the windowsill. Faith got up and followed him.

Down on the lawn, a lone fox stood, sniffing the air. Foxes were quite frequent visitors to the vicarage garden, hiding out under the overgrown shrubbery by the garden wall. Faith leaned out of the window to look more closely and the fox turned its head at the slight sound, and trotted back into the undergrowth. Faith felt the hairs on her arms rise. There was something about the creature that made her uneasy; the light grace with which it moved over the grass reminded her of Sal Hinkley.

Sal was so alive, so alert – just like the fox. Who would have been able to sneak up on her in her studio? She would have known if someone was there – she would have sensed a presence. But then – Faith's analytical brain was kicking in, as it did sometimes in the early hours – there were no signs of a struggle at the murder scene. The easel was upright, the paintbrush resting neatly on its stand. Sal wasn't frightened. She didn't feel threatened. Whoever came to her that night was *known* to her.

Faith shuddered at the thought, then picked up the cat and carried him back to the bed.

CHAPTER

4

On Wednesday morning, Faith was ready to start work at 6 a.m. which, considering the restless night she'd had, was pretty good. She collected up the notes she'd made for her foreword to the commemorative booklet and headed over to St James's, intending to sit in the cool of the vestry and finish off the writing before anyone else was up and about. But she wasn't the only early riser this morning. As she stepped out of the vicarage front door, she saw in the distance Fred's bent back in the new commemorative garden, and the flash of his spade as he laboured over yet another tree-hole.

It must be extraordinarily hard work digging when the ground was so parched and solid, especially for someone like Fred – a little overweight and definitely no longer in his prime. But it was never any use telling him to take it easy. If she said anything to that effect now, the churchwarden would simply point to the new young saplings lying on the lawn and tell her it was his duty to look after them – and if they weren't planted in the arbour today, they'd suffer – and he couldn't have that. Faith smiled. An alternative approach – some kind of distraction – was the only way to persuade him to take a break.

"Morning, Fred! You're making an early start. Very wise, in light of how hot it'll be later."

He straightened up, with a slightly shocked expression on his face which vanished when he made her out. "That's right, vicar," he said. "It's going to be a scorcher again."

"Come and have a cuppa," Faith said. 'I'm going to make one before I start work – and I'd really love some company."

"Well, I suppose if you twist my arm…" Fred gave her a shy smile.

They sat together in the vestry. Faith opted for the teapot, rather than bags in mugs, and the result was delicious. Fred gulped it down with relish.

"Tea's the best drink of all, when it's hot," he said. "Can't be doing with all that squash and stuff."

Now that she was close to him, Faith thought that he was looking a little strained, with puffy yellowish circles under his eyes. She asked him if he was all right.

"You look tired, Fred. Yesterday was a tough one, for all of us."

"Didn't sleep too well, I have to say."

"Me neither," Faith confessed.

"I kept seeing her…" Fred hesitated, his face drawn and unhappy.

"That's perfectly normal," Faith said. "We all had quite a shock." She couldn't banish the images from her own mind, either – Sal's body lying on the studio floor, with those dark bruises staining her neck. Faith herself was no stranger to the traumatic replay experience, after her years in the force. She'd attended many locations where violent crimes had taken place, and she'd seen bodies – both alive and dead – that had been subjected to horrific injuries: slashed faces; shattered limbs; the small, sinister slits of knife wounds. She'd had to view these with equanimity, pushing the natural reactions of revulsion and pity to the back of her mind. A crime scene was no place for emotion, for there was important work to be done, vital evidence to be collected and analysed. It was afterwards, when you were off-duty and relaxing that the horror of what you had seen hit you. Especially in the early hours, when you woke to those terrible images, sweating and shivering as you hadn't done when you were actually there.

The worst time for her had been after the death of a teenage boy who had been shot by a rival gang. Ben had been with her at the murder scene. He'd pointed out the neat, almost innocuous black mark in the smooth young skin, just to the side of the breastbone, where the bullet that killed the boy entered his body. Then the SOCO team had moved the corpse and revealed the mess where the bullet had exited through the boy's spine…

"Faith, are you OK?" Fred's hand brushed her knee. He was holding out her mug of tea, offering it to her. "You've gone a bit pale. Drink up!"

"I'm fine. Got a lot on my mind." She smiled and took the mug. The boy's death was one she would never forget – not just because of the horrific wound, and her helpless outrage at the waste of his young life – but because the boy's mother, Emilia Santa, had shown such extraordinary forgiveness towards the perpetrators. *It was hate that led to my son's death. Hate and ignorance. What good does it do in the world if I, too, am filled with hate?* Emilia's greatness of soul, her strength of spirituality in the face of mindless evil had become Faith's encounter on the road to Damascus. The turning point that led her here, to the incumbency of St James's church.

She turned to Fred.

"When you couldn't sleep, did you keep seeing her – Sal – again? As she was when you found her?"

"That's right." Fred shook his head. "Poor lass. Poor girl, lying there like that."

"Try not to dwell on it, Fred. It might help if you think of her when she was alive. She was a charismatic character, so vital and unique. Try to remember her like that, rather than picturing what happened to her."

Fred passed his handkerchief over his face. "I feel so bad," he said. "I never got to know her. She was there, right in the midst of us, all those weeks, and I don't think we ever spoke more than a couple of words to each other. I should have made more effort…"

Faith could have said the same. She had seen Sal flitting back and forth to the studio so often, and yet she knew almost nothing about her.

"She wasn't easy to get close to. I tried to chat to her several times, but she didn't seem to want to engage. She was a bit aloof, you might say."

Fred nodded. He drained the last of his tea and stood up. "Thank you, Faith. I'm much restored. I'd better get on."

He set off to resume digging in the arbour again, and Faith laid out her papers on the little table in the vestry. The foreword was beginning to come together quite well. She wrote on, oblivious to the passage of time, until footsteps hurrying over the stone flags of the church broke into her concentration. It was a shock to glance at her watch and see that it was 8:30. She had been writing for almost two hours.

Pat came bustling into the vestry, her mouth pursed with anxiety.

"Lock the doors!" she said.

"I'm sorry?" said Faith.

"Youths!" Pat spluttered. "Delinquents, loitering in our churchyard. One of them was trying to peer in through the window. Drug addicts, by the look of them, looking for easy pickings."

Faith got to her feet, perplexed. "Are they village kids?"

Pat shook her head and her cheeks quivered. "Absolutely not. They're here to look for things to steal. You should call your policeman friend. Get him to come and see them off."

"I'll go and talk to them," Faith said. It seemed a little unlikely that thieves would be casing the church for potential loot in broad daylight.

Pat looked doubtful, but she followed Faith out into the churchyard. A battered white van that had definitely seen better days was parked on the road, just outside the lychgate.

"See that?" Pat hissed in her ear. "Perfect for making a getaway."

Two teenage boys wearing ripped jeans and sloppy T-shirts stood on the path, looking around at the gravestones. Under one of the yew trees a girl with long blonde hair was sitting on the ground, leaning her back against the trunk. Nothing threatening about the three of them – they all seemed very relaxed.

"Careful!" Pat whispered, just behind Faith's shoulder as she made her way down the path. "I'm not at all sure we should engage with them."

"Morning," Faith called. "Can I help you?"

The taller of the two boys turned and looked at her. He had a sharp, thin face and lots of longish dark hair. "Hi," he said, holding out a hand. "The Reaches."

"Sorry?" Faith was stumped. For a moment she simply couldn't interpret what she'd just heard.

The boy grinned. "The band. We're booked to do a gig here, on Sunday. Aren't we?"

Ah! It all becomes clear.

"Of course!" Faith took his hand. There was a Post-it note somewhere, with the band's details on it, hidden in her pile of paperwork. She'd read a glowing write-up about them in the local paper, describing the band's performances in youth clubs and church halls – as well as some of their gigs in local clubs. *These guys are going places. Stunning vocals from Anya Lach, and a cool line-up from the guys on guitar and drums. Their Christian message packs a punch, too – it's contemporary and challenging. Unforgettable.*

"I'm so sorry," she said. "You're up very early, for musicians – I wasn't expecting you."

"No probs. You must be Faith Morgan, the vicar here." The boy had warm brown eyes. There was something very likeable about him, regardless of his rather scruffy attire.

"I am indeed. It was me that booked you – so I do apologize for forgetting your name. My only excuse, and it's not a very good one, is that I've had an awful lot on my mind with all the planning for the celebrations. And this is Pat – Pat Montesque. One of our churchwardens. You'll be seeing a lot of her on Sunday."

Faith looked round, expecting Pat to be still at her shoulder – but she had retreated to the safety of the porch, from where she was peering suspiciously at their conversation.

"Sweet!" the boy said, giving Pat a friendly wave. "Anya and Stevo and I have got lectures at eleven o'clock – we're taking the summer school course at our uni. So we thought we'd come down and check out the venue beforehand. Can we have a look round? We brought our gear down – the heavy stuff, amps and that. If we could drop some of it off now that would great. Oh – I'm Ethan, by the way."

"No problem," Faith said. "Nice to meet you, Ethan."

Anya jumped up from under the yew tree and came to join them. She was a tall girl with clear skin, and a full, sensual mouth. A silver ring had been inserted in her lower lip, which Faith found it hard not to focus on. Of course, piercings were commonplace these days, but they weren't seen too often among the congregation of St James's.

"Are we unloading?" Anya asked. Her voice had a clear, resonant quality – surprising in such a young woman. There was something silvery, almost bell-like about it.

"We certainly are," Ethan told her. "Oh – and this is Faith. She's the vicar. She booked us."

"Hey, that's great. Pleased to meet you," Anya said.

Fred must have heard their voices, for he had come up to look over the churchyard wall and see what was going on. Even Pat was emerging from the shadows of the porch.

"These guys are the star turn for Sunday evening," Faith called to him. "Could you give them a hand with their gear? They'd like to store some of their stuff in the church ready for Sunday."

"Of course!" Fred came ambling over.

"Are you sure this is good idea?" Pat muttered, as Anya and Ethan trundled a large wheeled case through the porch and into the church. "What if it gets stolen?"

Faith reassured her that everything could be safely left in the vestry.

"And the church is always locked at night. It will be fine, Pat."

46

"A pop group," Pat said, with a slight sniff, "at St James's. I never thought I'd see the day."

"Their songs have a strong message about the love of God, and their style of music reaches out to all, but especially to the young in the community," said Faith. "That's why they call themselves The Reaches. Because they want to reach out to everyone."

"Well. *Whatever* – as these young people say," Pat said, looking slightly mollified.

"Shall we go through the flower arrangements for Sunday?" Faith asked. This was not a priority – definitely not Post-it note status yet – but talk of floral decorations was normally enough to win Pat round.

"Oh, vicar, I'm afraid I can't just now," said the churchwarden. "Unfortunately. I've got a meeting with Jeremy at nine o'clock.'"

"*Another* one?" Fred said, coming past with an armful of cable drums. "What will the village gossips say?" He winked at Pat, who shook her head at him and hurried away towards the lychgate, her cheeks very pink.

"You shouldn't tease her, Fred," Faith said, when he came back from the vestry. "She doesn't quite know how to handle it. I think she's a bit sensitive where Jeremy's concerned."

"I know." Fred smiled. "They're inseparable, those two."

Faith nodded. Fred was far too mild-mannered to ever say what he really thought. Actually, he was probably too mild-mannered even to think anything amiss about the relationship between Pat and Jeremy Taylor. Still, she got the strong impression that Fred wasn't a huge fan of Jeremy. They were very different people – one, part of the fabric of the rural community, the other a newcomer who dressed the part but never quite convinced and, she had to admit, possessed something of an off-putting manner.

Faith let her eyes travel to the fields opposite the church. She could just see a crane on what was now Jeremy Taylor's land. There were upsides to having new money coming into the village.

"It's good to see the Shoesmith farm getting sorted out," she said.

Fred nodded sagely. "There's a bad feeling around there, I always think. And no wonder, when you think of how poor Trevor used to be, before he… well, you know." He paused and Faith tried not to let her memories stir. Trevor's body hanging in his barn. His loyal dog, finished off by Trevor's own hand with a shotgun blast.

The band's gear was stacked up in the vestry now, and there was nothing more to unload, so Fred set off back to his labours in the garden. Ethan and Anya wandered round the church, peering up at the newly restored stained-glass portrait of the Lamb of God and exclaiming over the carved wooden pews. Faith accompanied them, explaining where the power sockets were, and thinking how good it was to be with them as their youthful energy brought a new dynamism to the serene atmosphere of the old church.

For a random moment she found herself thinking of a pop festival she had visited once with Ben. Just for two days, staying in a tent. Ben had been extremely uncomfortable with the informality of it at first – said he hated the jostling bodies and the hysterical enthusiasm when the band came onto the stage. And all through the first band, he'd stood beside Faith like a block of wood. But an hour later he'd come out of himself and they'd danced together among the crowd, drunk on the night and the music. On the long drive home, he'd said they should do it again some time. They never had.

Anya was asking if she might test out the acoustic. When Faith agreed, she stood in front of the altar and sang a few lines of an old English folk song.

> *I leaned my back up against an oak, thinking that*
> *he was a trusty tree. But first he bended and then*
> *he broke – and so did my true love to me!*

Faith shivered at the sound of the girl's voice. The videos on YouTube hadn't done justice to its depth and clarity. Her interpretation, too, was wonderful – as she sang the simple melody, she was creating such sadness, such a sense of betrayal.

"You're very gifted," she said, when Anya had finished.

"Thanks. You're really kind," Anya smiled at Faith. "Don't worry, we'll use more upbeat stuff on Sunday."

"Have you thought of singing professionally? Your voice is fantastic. And it'll improve as you get older."

"I'm not sure, yet, what to do about my future," Anya said. "I'm just taking things one step at a time, with exams and everything. But thanks. Do you sing?"

"I used to," Faith said, remembering her moments of amateur glory in *My Fair Lady* and *Carousel*. "I just join in the hymns now, along with everyone else."

It was past ten thirty by the time the two young people had driven off in their van, rushing to get to their lecture. Faith was about to return to the vestry and carry on with her writing when she saw a movement in the paddock, close to Sal's studio hut. She felt an involuntary shiver.

A heavy-set man with broad, slightly stooped shoulders was standing close to the police tape. Definitely not an official, for he was wearing knee-length baggy shorts and a bright orange shirt. He reached out and twanged the tape with his hand. It looked as if at any moment he might try to climb over.

Faith hurried towards him across the churchyard.

"Hello, there! I'm Faith Morgan, the vicar of our church here. St James's. Can I help you?"

The man turned to her. He had a loose face, and curly grey hair that was thinning on top. He greeted her with a cursory nod and turned back towards the tape.

"Someone happened to mention that my wife had been murdered," he said, as if he was speaking of nothing more than the weather. "I thought I'd better pop over and see what's going on."

CHAPTER

5

"Your wife?" said Faith.

He turned round to face her again. His heavy cheeks drooped, giving him a rather sad, hangdog manner in spite of the smile which now crept over his face. He appeared to pick up on her unease. "I apologize," he said, drawing back the hand he was holding out for her to shake. "My humour is not appreciated by everyone. A bit too 'gallows', they tell me. I'll never learn."

His smile looked rather rueful now.

"Well, humour is a very personal thing," said Faith.

"I should introduce myself. I'm David McGarran," the man said, giving her a rather intense, searching look. His eyes were quite bloodshot, Faith noticed. "Sal was my wife."

Faith recalled talk of an ex-husband. "I see. Mr McGarran – I'm so very sorry for your loss."

"Ah, don't waste your sympathy." A shadow passed over David McGarran's loose, mobile face. He shook his head. "Sal walked out on me thirty years ago." He looked up towards the ramshackle studio. "So that was where she worked?"

"Yes," said Faith. "Every day for the last fortnight."

"And where she…?"

"Yes. That too."

McGarran grasped the striped police tape, and pushed it down.

"I don't think you should," Faith said, quickly. "The police may still be collecting evidence."

McGarran pulled the tape up tight and then let it go with a snap. "Ha! *The police.* They wasted eight hours last night interviewing me. *Eight hours*, would you believe. A full working-day's-worth of my life. And then the detective – or whatever he was – threatened to search both my home and the shop. For *evidence.* I told them they'd find nothing. What's to find, for God's sake? Excuse my blasphemy."

"It's quite all right," said Faith, feeling a sudden sympathy for the man. Another victim of Ben's slash-and-burn methods. She remembered his comments yesterday, about the high incidence of ex-partners being guilty in murder cases. No doubt he'd been interrogating McGarran with his usual disregard for anything except digging down to what he suspected was the unsavoury truth. Sal's ex-husband spoke as if he were trying to brush the whole thing off, but his words carried a sharp-edged defensiveness that belied his nonchalance. There was something painful buried under his casual exterior – an emotional instability that he was fighting hard to keep hidden.

"You're the governor of this gaff, so you say," McGarran jerked an eyebrow in the general direction of St James's.

"Indeed I am. Would you like to sit inside the church for a while? It's cool in there. You can relax, have some quiet time."

"No thanks. No." He looked back at the hut. A slight heat haze was rising from its corrugated iron roof, even though noon was still two hours away. "Not my thing," he added.

Faith knew she should get back to work, but she didn't like to leave McGarran. He had fallen quiet now, but his wide mouth was twisted a little, held tight as if he were trying to stifle that inner pain, whatever it might be. Perhaps it might help to ease some of his tension and satisfy her own curiosity, which in spite of herself was really niggling – if they spoke some more about his wife.

As it was, he broke the silence.

"She came to see me, you know? A few days ago."

Faith offered an expression of interest rather than surprise. "How was it?"

"Oh, she was just Sal, of course. What else? She walked in as if we'd seen each other just a few weeks ago. Like nothing had happened."

"That must have been hard for you."

He shrugged. "You know what? I was surprised to see her, out of the blue like that, but what was I going to say? Tell her off, for walking out? It was thirty years ago. Past history."

The defensiveness was back. Probably wiser to back off, to let the subject drop.

The big man gave a dismissive snort. "You're a lot less nosy than the police, you know."

Faith nodded. "I'm not investigating a murder."

McGarran smiled a little. "Funny, the detective could never ask one question at a time. Always two, or three, quick-fire, like he didn't really want the answers and just wanted to confuse me. *Why did she leave you? Why were you so angry at Sal?*"

McGarran might not be a churchgoer, but Faith knew when she was being taken into confidence. She couldn't help herself.

"Why didn't it work out between you?"

"I don't know," said McGarran. "I never got to the bottom of it. I assumed she was having an affair. That she went out to Australia to be with *him*, whoever he was. But apparently she lived on her own out there. So your guess is as good as mine."

He turned away from Faith and looked over at St James's, standing solid and ancient amid the yew trees. A tremor passed over his face.

"I used to come here, when I was a little kiddie," he said. "Back in the sixties. My dad knew the old vicar. We used to come most Sundays."

He clearly wanted to prolong their conversation.

"What a coincidence. I came here too, as a child. My father was a bell-ringer. He would bring my sister and me along when he came to St James's for a session. He'd take us to the pub afterwards and buy us a shandy. We used to feel so grown up."

"There's a thing," McGarran said. He gave a little sigh, as if in regret for the lost happiness of the past.

Over at Shoesmith's old farm the chainsaw coughed and roared into life, shattering the peace. McGarran flinched at the harsh sound. It seemed to be causing him some distress. His eyes rolled upwards in a brief expression of horror.

"Are you all right?"

McGarran blinked, refocusing on Faith. "I think perhaps I *should* go and have a look round the church. Why not?"

As they walked over the pasture to the churchyard he said, with a long face, "I've no alibi for the night of Sal's death, you see. The detective inspector kept harping on about it. I live alone. Well – except for my old Monty. But I don't think the testimony of an aged Jack Russell will count for much, do you?"

He looked so tragically gloomy as he said this that it took Faith a moment to realize that he had just made another of his rather awful jokes.

Once inside the church, McGarran seemed to pick up a little. He walked along the nave with his head held high, looking up into the roof vault.

"This is a beautifully proportioned building," he said. "Look at those timbers. They knew their stuff, those old carpenters. Lovely work."

"I agree. It's a most wonderful church. I feel lucky, every day, that I work here," Faith said.

McGarran came to a halt. "Is Sal's painting about? The commission? I'd like to see it."

Faith explained that the painting was still with the police. "It's a shame, David. I'm sorry it's not here. I had a brief glimpse of it." And that's all it had been, really, with the body there and all. "It's a very striking composition."

"I daresay. She can make a point, Sal. Not scared to put herself on the line with her work. Bit close to the bone sometimes, for me, but it went down well with the critics." McGarran dug in the pocket of his shorts and pulled out a dog-eared business card to give to Faith. "This is me," he said. "If you need anything framed, any time. Etchings, school photographs, saucy postcards, whatever you like."

Faith thanked him.

McGarran looked around at the church again. "To be honest, I'm surprised she took the commission," he said. "Hardly Sal's thing, religion. Well, must dash."

Faith watched him go. She would like to have spent some time mulling over their conversation, which seemed to have raised more questions than it had answered, but it was almost lunchtime. She must grab a snack, and then put the finishing touches to her foreword for the booklet. McGarran's comments about Sal "putting herself on the line" had struck a chord. A little more personal disclosure about Faith's own journey to becoming the vicar of St James's would really bring the piece to life.

Faith lifted her head from the scatter of papers on the little table in the vestry. Something had broken the bubble of her concentration. Not a noise, but its opposite – a sudden silence. The distant, irritating buzz of the chainsaw, a constant accompaniment all the while she had been working, had finally ceased. The builders must be taking a tea break. She put down her pen, stretching out her cramped fingers. It was so much easier working out her ideas on paper than tapping away at the laptop. The foreword was done now, and all that remained was to type it up and print it out.

Change was her subject. Change, and all the challenge that it brings – along with the potential for spiritual growth. She'd had no problem writing about the cataclysmic waves of change that the stalwart stone church had endured. The Reformation. The Civil War. The terrible conflicts and losses of the twentieth century's two world wars. Yet St James's was still here, strengthened by adversity, its walls steeped in a spirituality that would bring succour to those who must suffer whatever tribulations lay ahead in this new young century.

The painful transitions she, Faith Morgan, had undergone to achieve spiritual growth had been a little harder to put down on paper. But she was happy with the final result. A few candid touches had brought life and humour to the writing. She smiled, rereading her description of the pilgrimage she had made to the shrine of St James at Santiago de Compostela in Spain, shortly after she had made the decision to leave the force and commit to a life within the church.

She had begun her gruelling walk along the Camino Frances on the French side of the Pyrenees, where she joined ranks with some other pilgrims – a group of theology students who were also keen hikers. Faith was pretty fit after her years in the police, but she wasn't accustomed to walking such long distances over tough terrain, and her feet were soon badly blistered. The students hung around with her for a day or so, walking just a few miles at her slow pace, but she was clearly holding them back, so she told them to go on ahead while she made her own way. The pain in her feet was excruciating, but she embraced it. Her one indulgence was her make-up kit. Looking well presented had been an integral part of her routine as a policewoman. The right shade of lipstick, a subtle but flattering eyeshadow, had played an important role in keeping her morale up through the long, gruelling shifts and the inevitable stresses of interacting with difficult and sometimes abusive people. It was a habit that was deeply ingrained.

At the start of the pilgrimage, in her low budget accommodation along the route, Faith took time each morning to apply a layer of foundation, a dash of mascara, and a touch of bright lipstick. As she hobbled over the stones of the Camino, she was, at least, facing the world with a semblance of good grooming. Gradually Faith's feet toughened up and the blisters healed. But one morning, staying in a youth hostel just across the Spanish border, she woke to find her make-up bag gone. Someone had taken it while she slept.

So Faith had to tramp on, sweaty-faced and swollen-eyed, without the solace of her mask. Her one remaining indulgence was to put on fresh underwear and a clean T-shirt every day. And then, just four days away from Santiago, her backpack was stolen, and she was left with the clothes she stood up in. When she finally stood beneath the rugged, imposing frontage of the cathedral of St James the Great, Faith was grubby, exhausted and not at all, in her opinion, "nice to know". And it didn't matter a jot. The experience of unconditional love as she entered the deeply spiritual ambience of the shrine of St James was never to be forgotten. All that mattered was that she, Faith, was there. Walking through the ancient cloisters, sitting quietly in the gardens to meditate, she saw, so clearly, the life ahead of her. A path of love and service that required no external fripperies, no presentation, just herself, her heart and soul. She knew, then, that she had made the right choice – and that whether she believed herself worthy or not she was held within a love that was eternal and infinite.

Faith tidied up the papers and clipped them together. The moment within the cathedral would never leave her. It was there, deep inside, to be accessed whenever she felt unequal to her role – or questioned the strength of her belief. She found her thoughts straying to Sal again. McGarran had stated that the artist wasn't religious. So what had impelled her to make her own epic pilgrimage to the other side of the world and back? Was it her art? A creative impulse that could not be denied, impelling her to cut loose and head for the burning skies and the vast red deserts of Australia? Or was it, as McGarran had initially suspected, love? A passion so strong that all else was burnt out from her soul?

Someone was tapping on the door of the vestry. Faith had been so engrossed in her thoughts that she hadn't heard anybody coming in to the church.

"Come in!"

Sergeant Peter Gray's head appeared around the vestry door.

"Got something for you!" he said. He held up a large, bubble-wrapped oblong. Faith's heart skipped a beat. It must be Sal's painting!

"Had to bribe the guys in the evidence room," he continued, with a wink.

"Peter!"

He grinned. "Not really, don't panic. They've dusted it for fingerprints. Nothing on there but the victim's, so they've let it go."

"Thank you so much, Peter. Very thoughtful of you to bring it over so quickly. It's a shame, the artist's ex-husband was here earlier. He'd have liked to see it."

Peter looked surprised. "McGarran came by? Really? I'd have thought he'd have kept away after the grilling Ben gave him yesterday."

"I did get the impression he'd had rather a hard time of it."

"Yup. The boss was convinced he was hiding something. And he's got no alibi. We've got nothing else on him though. Much as the boss hates to concede – McGarran's probably not our man."

"Man?" Faith interrupted. She couldn't help herself. "You're making some assumptions there, aren't you? What makes you think the killer was male?"

Peter's gaze sharpened, and she wished she had kept quiet.

"What's this about?" he asked in a much more formal tone. "You said that as if you know something, Faith. Something you haven't shared?"

"No, no."

It was a very awkward moment – a sudden clash of worlds. Peter was a member of Faith's flock. A warm, friendly presence to interact with in church. All of a sudden he had become impersonal, assertive. Adopting his professional stance.

"I was just – being logical, Peter," she said, as gently as she could. "Looking at the bigger picture. It's never wise to jump to conclusions."

"Right, OK." Peter looked slightly embarrassed. He continued in a more conversational tone: "Maybe I should put you in the picture with where we are on the case. Sal's hyoid bone was snapped. It takes a lot of force to do that. So it's possibly more likely to have been a male that killed her. First up we thought whoever strangled her used their hands, but the bruising pattern isn't consistent with fingers."

A chill ran down Faith's spine. That shed a very different light on the events in the artist's hut. This might not be a spur-of-the-moment *crime passionnel*, but something far more sinister. A cold-blooded killing.

"So you think this was premeditated?"

"Absolutely." Peter pulled out his notebook and checked through the entries in it. "And forensics think she was killed before 10 p.m. So that's a pretty narrow window when the crime could have taken place. Run it past me again, Faith – when did you see her going to the hut?"

His tone was still light, but there was an edge. And he wasn't looking her in the eye.

"At seven. Just a few moments after the clock struck. I've told Ben. He's got all the details."

"Ah, great. The boss is clued up. Right." Peter snapped the notebook shut. "I'd better get on. Thanks, Faith, for everything."

"No, thank you, Peter. It was really kind of you to bring the painting."

He grinned at her, his usual affable self once more, and left the vestry.

Sal probably died at dusk, Faith thought. As the sun went down. The artist's life was crushed out of her as the long, hot day ended. A bleak, empty feeling descended on her, and to push it away she pulled out her phone and sent a text. *Hello Pat! Great news! The painting for the cover is here! I'll take to the printers and get it scanned this afternoon. Faith.*

She waited a moment but there was no reply. Pat was usually extremely swift in getting back to her – a late adopter of texting, but an enthusiastic one. She must be busy and have put her phone down somewhere out of earshot.

Faith turned to the painting. Peter had done a good job of packing the canvas, and it took her a long while to unstick the Sellotape he had wound round to keep the bubble wrap tight.

As she carefully peeled away the last sheet of bubble wrap, Faith had to step back and take a breath. It was one thing to have gained a brief impression of the work when she saw it propped on the easel at the murder scene – but to have it here, right in front of her! The effect was electric. With bold, sweeping brushstrokes Sal had portrayed the stalwart shape of St James's, dwarfed by a swirling mass of iron-grey and inky black storm clouds. Just one ray of brilliant light broke through the heavy skies, creating a slash of vivid green where it fell in the churchyard.

The image was more moving than anything she could have imagined. Something about the looming, tumultuous clouds reminded her of the apocalyptic engravings of the Victorian religious artist, John Martin – but the painting's energy, its vibrant colour were absolutely contemporary. Sal had perfectly captured the essence of the old church building – there was a gentle light, a steady radiance which seemed to emanate from the ancient stonework – so that you felt, as you looked at it, that there was a glimmer of hope St James's might survive the storm that threatened. The all-engulfing storm that loomed in the sky. And that beam of light, shining down on the churchyard – Faith felt a rush of emotion as she looked at it. There was something intensely poignant about the sliver of brightness piercing the black clouds and illuminating the greenness of the hallowed ground below.

Sal might not have put much store in the life of the church, or God, but Faith realized in that moment that he had worked through her. The sacred, transcendent aspect of art was something Ben, for one, had never understood.

Faith touched the surface of the paint lightly. For all that she had barely spoken to the artist, she couldn't help but feel a connection now, seeing her church through the painter's clear eyes.

"Thank you," Faith said. "Thank you, Sal."

CHAPTER

6

"It's Faith!" Daniel Wythenshaw said, enveloping Faith in a passionate bear hug. "Hello, Faith!"

Daniel was all of six feet two inches tall, and very strong with it, but his embrace was heartfelt and innocent. Faith recalled the way her nephew Sean had greeted her as a boy with unbridled joy.

"Put our lovely vicar down, Daniel," his mother, Bella, said, in an affectionate tone. "Not everybody appreciates being swept off their feet like that. Shake hands and say how-do-you-do. That's the proper way to greet somebody."

"I don't mind at all. It's nice to have such a warm welcome – though I guess your mum is right," Faith said, extricating herself from Daniel's arms and offering her hand to be shaken.

She had dropped by at the River Lodge B&B on her way to the printers, hoping to check up on how the Wythenshaws were coping with the aftermath of Sal's violent death. Hard to believe that the artist had been living under this roof until a couple of days ago.

"How-de-do!" Daniel said, grinning and shaking her hand with gusto.

"I'm very well, thank you. And yourself? How do you do?" Faith replied, in a very formal tone, much to Daniel's delight. He doubled over with giggles, too amused to respond.

"So kind of you to call in," Bella said, brushing a loose strand of her curly hair back from her forehead. "I can imagine how busy you must be right now, with the anniversary celebrations at the weekend. Have you got time for tea? The kettle's boiling."

"Tea! And cake!" Daniel slapped his midriff.

"There isn't any cake," Bella told him. "Not today, my love."

Daniel's face fell and he made a spluttering noise of disapproval.

His mother ignored this. In the same warm, positive tone she said: "If you'd like to bring a chair for Faith, you can have a biscuit."

The incredible patience, kindness and devotion that Daniel's parents always showed towards their son never ceased to inspire Faith. Their unfailing love and their consistent, careful management of his sometimes difficult behaviour had reaped rich rewards. He was a lively, high-spirited young man, and yet always polite and thoughtful. Right now he was carrying a chair over to Faith, and he held it carefully for her while she sat down.

"Thank you, Daniel."

"You're *welcome*," he replied with a beaming smile.

"I've made a pot of tea." Gavin Wythenshaw, Daniel's father, came through from the kitchen. "I assume that's what the kettle was for?"

The B&B was a tightly run operation; everybody pulled their weight, including Daniel. He followed his mother to the kitchen now, ready to help her carry the tea things.

"It's good to see you, Gavin," Faith said. "I can't stay long – I'm up against it today, what with all the arrangements for Sunday. I just wanted to come by and make sure that you're all right, all of you."

"Bit in shock still, to be honest," Gavin said. "The police have turned Sal's room upside down. They took all her stuff away, too. It's all been so sudden. One minute she was here – and the next there's no trace of her." He shook his head. There were dark circles under his eyes, as if he hadn't slept too well, and he was chewing his bottom lip. He looked ill at ease.

"It's a shock for all of us," Faith said, and then waited in case he wanted to say anything more. He did.

"I feel so guilty," he sighed.

"Why?" Faith asked gently, in a neutral tone. There was a clink of crockery from the kitchen, and a roar of laughter from Daniel. Bella was talking to him, but Faith couldn't make out what she was saying.

"I should have checked up on her," Gavin said, in a low voice. "She didn't come down to breakfast, and I never thought to go up and check to see if she'd come back that night. I should have done. She was our guest; it was my responsibility to do that. We just thought she'd got up early and gone off to the studio. But..." he hesitated.

"What is it?"

The conversation was interrupted by the return of Daniel and Bella with the tea tray. Daniel took his mug of tea, grabbed a biscuit and headed off to his room to enjoy them in peace.

Bella fussed with the mugs and the teapot. Gavin gave her

an anxious look, and then said, "Well, she kept strange hours, you know? Going out at funny times."

"It's not your job to make sure your guests are in bed," said Faith. Bella passed round the mugs of tea and then stayed standing up to drink hers, leaning on the table with a preoccupied air.

"See," she said. "You're not to blame, Gav."

Faith sipped her tea and almost burnt her lip. "How was Sal, the last few days?" she asked. "Did you notice anything different about her?"

"No. But then – she never gave a thing away," Gavin said. "Kept herself to herself."

The same story. The artist's emotions – whatever was happening in her inner world – were impenetrable to those around her.

Bella was staring down into her mug as if there was something unpleasant at the bottom of it. Clearly she had her own thoughts about Sal. Faith was not here, though, to interrogate the Wythenshaws but to support them. She had done quite enough questioning for someone whose role was a pastoral one. She thanked them for the tea before it was half finished and stood up to take her leave, citing her schedule.

On her way out to the car a few moments later, Faith found herself alone in the hallway with Gavin.

"Is Bella all right? She looked a bit... upset when we were talking about Sal just then. It's not good to suppress your emotions at a time like this."

Gavin took a step closer to her. "Sal wasn't the easiest guest," he said, in a low voice. "To be honest, we rather regretted having her to stay. She was downright rude to Bella a couple of times."

"Oh? What do you mean?"

Gavin shifted a little uneasily, casting a glance back along the hall. "It might seem silly to you, but we have a policy here that breakfast is between seven thirty and nine thirty. There's a lot to do, running a business like this. There's a bit of flexibility, obviously – but this one morning, Sal came swanning down at ten wanting a full English, and we couldn't do it. We had to take Daniel into Winchester for a check-up. She flew off the handle with Bella. It was completely out of order."

"I'm so sorry to hear that," said Faith. "It doesn't sound like you were being unreasonable."

Gavin glanced over his shoulder and moved closer. "Apart from anything else, Daniel gets upset if there are raised voices. It unsettles him, especially if his mum's involved. He gets very protective – you know?"

Faith nodded. It was understandable. Daniel was a sensitive boy, and quite emotional. Of course he would be anxious if he felt Bella was being threatened.

"And another time…" Gavin continued "… this was in the early hours of the morning – Sal was marching up and down the landing outside her room shouting at someone on her mobile. One of the other guests came out and asked her to be quiet. She started yelling at *him*. Woke everybody up. Daniel, too. It was mayhem. Absolute chaos."

"You've told the police all this?" Faith's limbs were tingling with adrenaline.

"Yes – though we tried to play it down as much as possible. It's nothing to do with us – what happened to her. And – we don't want it getting around, Faith. We've got a business to run. Anything that might put people off from staying here…"

Faith nodded sympathetically and said farewell, then went out to the car feeling distinctly troubled. It was extremely hot inside. Just that half hour parked up in the full sun had transformed the Yaris into an oven. She got in and wound the windows down, looking out at the smooth surface of the River Itchen winding lazily past the B&B. This was a perfect spot for keen anglers and hikers to base themselves. Gavin and his wife would normally have no problem getting bookings, but she understood his concern. To be linked, even tangentially, to a murder victim, couldn't be a good thing.

The Wythenshaws were reasonable, kind people. She found it hard to imagine them ever not getting on with their typical guests, who'd be happy to be looked after in tranquil surroundings, exchanging pleasantries over breakfast and asking for advice on the local area. But that was the thing about Sal – she was hardly a typical guest.

All that anger, the shouting – the complete reverse of her normally withdrawn, rather isolated persona. Pretty much all of the time, Sal had been monosyllabic and detached when Faith had spoken to her.

Apart from one time, of course.

It hadn't been face to face, thank goodness, but still – Faith had found herself on the receiving end of Sal's anger, and it was particularly unpleasant.

Faith drummed her fingers on the steering wheel. She'd rather pushed the incident to the back of her mind. Always best not to dwell on upsetting things, especially when there was so much work to do. But after what Gavin had said, what had happened three days ago was replaying again, clear and sharp as when it occurred.

Very early on Monday morning a week ago, Faith had been

in the rectory kitchen in her dressing gown, pouring milk over a bowl of cereal. She'd heard a loud bang – that unmistakeable metallic *crack* of one vehicle hitting another – right outside the vicarage gate. When she ran out to see what had happened, Sal's green estate car was speeding away up the road at a fair pace. And on the front wing of Faith's Yaris was a swathe of dented, scratched metal. How could Sal not have noticed that she'd bumped the car? She must have felt the collision – and the dent was plain to see.

Head spinning with the unexpectedness of it all, Faith had run out into the road and waved, but the estate car didn't stop. Shock was quickly replaced by anger. *How dare she just drive away?* She ran inside and found Sal's number on the mobile. She couldn't make the call, though, not right then. It was too early in the morning, and she was too shocked and upset. Her brain simply wouldn't compute what she might say. The occasion called for assertiveness, but something about Sal – her reserve, her complete disregard for the niceties of human interaction – made Faith feel nervous and uncertain. It was lunchtime before she could bring herself to try again, but when she rang the call had gone straight through to Sal's voicemail and she had to leave a message.

Sal called her back at 11:30 that night. Faith was in her night things, cleaning her teeth. She hurried out of the bathroom, wiping toothpaste from her mouth, and picked up the phone.

"You've got a cheek," Sal had said, without any attempt at a greeting. Her voice was cold. "Accusing me like that."

Faith explained that she had seen the artist's car driving away.

"Really? Perhaps you should get your eyes tested. I was nowhere near your house this morning."

Anger surged in Faith.

"You must have heard the crunch when you hit my car."

"Don't insult my intelligence," Sal said. And then she swore at Faith, in the same cold, colourless tone. "You stupid cow," she said. "Just get off my back." And then she cut the call.

Faith was shaking as she went through to the bedroom. It wasn't just those vile words – she had heard far worse as a policewoman. It was the icy bitterness with which Sal had spoken them.

Faith had debated with herself what to do next. Phoning the police would have been time-consuming. Sal's car would certainly have some damage as well, though ascribing it to the collision might not be straightforward. Plus, there was principle at stake. But the longer she dwelled on it, the more her anger subsided.

Such bitterness must surely come from pain, her inner voice had said, calm and clear inside her head. *Sal's upset about something. Perhaps she was upset this morning, too, which is why she drove away. Perhaps she was so distressed that she didn't even notice what she had done. Her words, her cruel tone – they can't have been anything to do with you.*

At once Faith had been struck with a flood of compassion for Sal. A pain that could crack such a tough, reserved exterior must be devastating. She had knelt by the bed and prayed for the artist, sending heartfelt wishes for her peace of mind. As she prayed, she came to the decision to not pursue the matter further. If Sal was under a lot of emotional stress, it wasn't worth adding to it. The Yaris was a good few years old now, and maybe the man in Winchester who serviced it for Faith would be able to beat out the dent for a reasonable cost. She had prayed for more than half an hour, and when at last she fell into bed she had released all her anger and had put the horrible moment when Sal swore at her right out of her mind. When she saw the artist on Monday night, walking over the pasture to the hut, Sal had seemed her usual self again. Her car, Faith noticed, had several dents – perhaps she was a particularly poor driver.

And Faith had done such a good job of "letting go" that the incident had completely slipped her mind yesterday, when she had been at the crime scene.

Ben would be furious with her, she thought, as she sat in the hot car, watching the river slide slowly by. It had all happened the morning of the day that Sal died. Should she have told him? Yes, of course. *So why didn't you?* asked her inner voice.

Faith turned the key in the ignition to start the engine and get the aircon going. *She* knew it wasn't relevant to the case, but Ben wouldn't see it that way. And was there perhaps a tiny part of her that perversely enjoyed knowing something he didn't? But how long would it be before they worked out the angry call Gavin had heard was to Faith?

The sooner she told Ben the better. Faith pulled out onto the road.

CHAPTER

7

It was very hot in the printing shop and the air was thick with photocopier fumes. Faith sat by the open door on a wobbly plastic chair that felt as if it was in imminent danger of total collapse, waiting for the scan of the painting to be completed. Despite trying to reassure herself, Ben was in the forefront of her mind. She could call him right now on the mobile and come clean about her row with Sal, but it was going to be such a difficult conversation that it might be wiser to go back to the vicarage and call him on the landline. That way she would be more grounded, and better able to deal with whatever accusations he might throw at her.

"All done, vicar." The printer, a stout man with a sheen of sweat on his forehead, came through from the back of the shop with the painting. "Bit doom and gloom, this. I thought you'd want something a bit more cheerful for your booklet."

"I rather like it," Faith said. "It seems to reflect some of the challenges that the church faces in these difficult times."

The printer smiled at her. "Well, you're the expert!"

With the canvas safely wrapped and replaced in the rear

seats of the car, Faith headed back to Little Worthy. There was not much traffic on the roads, as it was now the middle of the afternoon. Along the narrow back lane into the village she spotted the flash of two bright yellow hi-viz jackets up ahead. A pony and rider were coming towards her, accompanied by a pedestrian. Faith put her foot on the brake and pulled over to a halt on the verge. Always best to deploy maximum caution where horses were concerned – they could be very unpredictable.

She waited as the trio approached. On first sighting, she'd assumed that the pony – a long-legged grey – was in the charge of a couple of girls from the local riding school. Now that she was stationary, and could take a proper look, she realized that the figure at the pony's head was actually a tall man of imposing build. It was Timothy Johnston, a barrister from one of the law firms in Winchester and the head of Little Worthy's only black family. He and his wife, Clarisse, were among Faith's most loyal parishioners. His young daughter, Emily, was sitting proudly in the saddle, a broad smile on her face.

The pony tossed its head and sidled as they approached the car, and Timothy spoke to it in an authoritative tone, hanging on tight to the lead rein.

"Hello, you two!" Faith called, winding down her window as they drew level.

The pony was very striking. It was dark grey – the colour of tarnished silver, with white dapples over its sides and rump. The effect reminded Faith of the sheen on a tarnished silver bowl that lurked in the back of one of the cupboards in the vestry.

"He's a rather splendid pony, Emily. What's his name?" Faith asked.

"Eligius!" Emily grimaced as she said this.

Faith frowned. She wondered if she'd misheard. "That's a very unusual name for a pony."

"Emily wants to rename him," said Timothy, "but we thought it might be better not to confuse him for the moment."

Faith smiled. She was a little surprised to see that the reins Emily was holding were bright pink. As was the strap around the pony's brow, which was studded with diamante, rather like the collar of a pampered pooch. The colour went with the pony's silvery coat, but Faith had never seen a pony wear pink before. She was about to remark on this, but Timothy was talking.

"St Eligius is the patron saint of horses," he explained, patting the animal's sleek neck. Faith noticed that he was wearing thick gloves, a rather odd choice for such a hot day. "Emily's mad about riding," he continued. "We've done a deal with the stables. If she grooms this chap and cleans out his stable four nights in the week, she can have four rides on him. She wants her own pony, eventually – and this way she'll learn about the responsibilities that go along with it. It's not all fun, is it, pet?"

Emily grinned. "I don't mind shovelling up the poo!" she said, with a cheeky look at Faith. "And Eligius is so pretty, I love brushing him. D'you like his new reins, Faith?" She lifted up her hands, showing off the bright pink leather.

"I do," Faith said. "Pink rather suits him."

"Emily paid for them out of her own pocket money," Timothy explained.

"I've got the reins and the brow band, and I'm going to get him a whole new pink bridle, when I've saved up enough," said Emily. "And a pink saddlecloth. And I'm going to give him a new name. Diamond. All the ponies at the stables have their own special nickname. That can be his," Emily said. She was clearly completely besotted with her new equine friend.

"Lovely to see you both – and to meet Eligius," Faith said. "Or Diamond, I should say. I must be getting back."

"Of course." Timothy raised a hand to wave goodbye. Once again Faith was struck by the incongruity of the heavy gloves he was wearing.

"Those look warm," she commented. "Aren't they rather uncomfortable today?"

Timothy frowned. "They help me get a grip. This chap can be a bit obstreperous. Especially in the traffic. That's why I've come out with Emily today. Just to help her get used to managing him." He flexed his gloved fingers on the lead rein.

"Ah, I see. Well – goodbye for now. Enjoy your ride, Emily."

"Thank you," the girl said, pressing her heels into the pony's sides. "I'll be fine, Daddy. I can ride him really well."

"Best to be on the safe side," Timothy countered, hanging on with both hands as Eligius bounded past the car.

When the trio were about twenty yards away, Faith turned the key in the ignition. As she drove off she saw in her mirror that the pony was swinging across the tarmac, throwing his head up as Timothy tugged on the lead rein. Emily didn't look too bothered by the misbehaviour of her mount; her head was held high as the pony pranced along the lane, its stippled coat gleaming in the sunshine.

Glory be to God for dappled things, Faith thought, as a long-ago school poetry lesson surfaced in her mind. Gerard Manley Hopkins, of course. The Catholic priest who was also a poet. And the poem? "Pied Beauty", written in 1918. It occurred to her that if there were an Olympics of Trivial Pursuit, she might well be a candidate. It was just a shame that the more important stuff – like the messages on the Post-it notes – didn't always come to mind with such ease.

Faith parked up on the vicarage drive. As she locked the driver door she looked down at the dent in the side of the Yaris. There was a ragged scrape of green paint from Sal's car there. *Right. You cannot postpone the moment of disclosure any longer!* She picked up Sal's wrapped canvas from the gravel and turned to go into the house. *I won't even let you make a detour via the kitchen to put the kettle on – you're going straight to the phone to call Peter...*

As she approached the porch, a tall figure stepped out in front of her. Ben. Her heart gave a flutter in her chest. How long had he been waiting for her?

"You took your time." He raised one dark eyebrow at her.

"I'm sorry," Faith said, and immediately felt ridiculous. *Why should I apologize? I didn't know he was here. And he knows I'm busy – that I have a job to do, even if it's not one that he can see the point of...*

"I need a word with you." Ben's tone was chilly. "About the call history on the Hinkley woman's mobile. The guys've been checking through it."

This wasn't the bluster she'd been dreading. Yet Ben's cool, controlled manner might be masking an anger that could erupt at any moment if she said the wrong thing.

"And of course my number came up." Faith took care to keep her tone a match for his – calm and neutral. "Why don't you come in?"

Half an hour and several glasses of mineral water and Rose's Lime Juice later, and Ben was leaning his elbows on the scrubbed-pine kitchen table, chin resting on his hands. He hadn't seemed entirely convinced by Faith's account of her conversation with Sal. Yet – thank goodness – he seemed more puzzled than angry.

"I don't get it," he said. "This isn't *you*. Absolutely not the woman I know." He gave a little exasperated sigh. "Or perhaps I should say, the woman I *thought* I knew. Why on earth didn't you follow this up? Sal Hinkley damaged your car. This should be put through the proper channels, and then you can make an insurance claim."

"I'm sorry, Ben. It's just…" Faith hesitated. Impossible to tell him her real reason for not pursuing an insurance claim. He would never comprehend her moment of compassion for the pain that she'd sensed in Sal. She decided to appeal to his logical side instead – a lie, but a white one at least.

"Look at it from my point of view," she said. "Sal had been chosen to paint a very important picture of the church. Chosen, I should add, after painful debate. If I rocked the boat by accusing her of fleeing the scene of a motor accident, that could have thrown the whole commission into jeopardy."

Ben was shaking his head in disbelief.

"Look," she continued. "I know this will seem infuriatingly silly to you, but it just didn't feel like the right thing to do."

Ben frowned, leaning forward over the kitchen table. "That's so out of character as to make me doubt your sanity," he said. "You were the hardest cop of all on the driving offences when you worked traffic. What's going on with you?"

His blue eyes fixed on hers – but not with the interrogative ferocity that she'd feared. With something very different – a sudden anxiety. *He's concerned for me! I'm not sure I can handle this. It's too confusing.* Faith looked down at the melting ice in the bottom of her glass.

"What's up?" Ben asked, after a pause.

Her skin felt suddenly clammy. Those horrible words that Sal used. *You stupid cow.* She didn't want to tell Ben, not because he'd be angry; she couldn't handle him getting all protective on her behalf. It was too confusing, him being like that. She had to find a way to put him off the scent, dilute the intensity of the hot blue stare that was boring into her skull.

"It was different then, Ben. It was my job as traffic cop to keep the roads a safe place for the public. To be honest, I suppose with Sal I – didn't want to cause trouble."

"Fay." Ben wasn't giving up. "That's not it. There's something else. Isn't there?"

He knew her too well. Faith knotted her fingers together under the table. Ben wouldn't back off. She would have to give a little more ground. The artist's icy, cruel voice, quiet and venomous, echoed again in her head.

"Listen, Ben – I can say this much. Sal seemed somewhat stressed when I spoke to her. I didn't know what was going on. And it was just a little prang, after all."

Ben leaned back. "So she was stressed, was she? I bet she gave you an earful."

Faith nodded. *Why was it – after all this time – that he could still read her so easily?*

"Yes. You could say that. She was very upset about something. And she – took it out on me."

Ben's face darkened a little. He was irritated with her – was probably thinking, *Why is she being so bloody charitable again? Wasting so much sympathy on those who don't deserve it? Saint Faith… or so she'd like to see herself.*

"You've put me in a difficult position," he said, after a moment. "I can't pretend I didn't hear what you just told me. You'll have to give an official statement."

Faith's stomach tightened. "Is that really necessary?"

Ben raised an eyebrow at her. "You were the last person to see Sal alive. And on paper, at least, you've got every reason to hold a grudge against her. She bashed a dent in your car and drove off, and she was rude to you over the phone. She seemed – as you say – wound up about something. This has to have some relevance to the case. It ain't rocket science, Fay."

"No. It's not. I suppose I should come down to the station tomorrow?"

Ben nodded. "Ten o'clock?"

"Yes, that's fine," Faith said. At least she would have a couple of hours beforehand in which to catch up with some of the tasks on her clipboard. Then she remembered. "Actually, no, it isn't. Sorry, Ben. I've got to take my mother up to London for a medical appointment. With a consultant. I need to pick her up from Ruth's around nine thirty. Could you fit me in any earlier?"

Ben pushed his chair back and stood up, rolling his eyes to the heavens. The gesture was exaggerated, for effect.

Faith waited, feigning hopeful expectation, but she already knew what he'd say.

"All right," he said, quite amicably. "Seven thirty do it for you?"

"Perfect."

"I'll bring you a bacon butty," he said, with a half-smile. A favourite treat of theirs, back in the day when they were on the early morning shift. "How is Marianne, by the way?"

"She's good at the moment," Faith said. Best not to get

involved in a conversation about the possibility of dementia. "It's just a check-up. Thanks for asking."

"Give her my best."

He went, shoving his chair under the long table and pulling the kitchen door to behind him.

Faith was left to put together a salad for her supper while she tried to work out which of two emotions – sadness or an odd, unexpected joy – was affecting her most strongly.

CHAPTER

8

"Hospitals are much nicer places than they used to be. Look!" Marianne pointed at a framed poster of Monet's *Water Lilies* that hung above the reception desk in the dementia clinic waiting room. "We could be sitting in the lobby of a hotel."

"That's a very positive take on it," Faith replied. "I'm not sure I'd go that far."

The clinic was located on the tenth floor of an ultra-modern tower block that formed part of the hospital site. The view that stretched away over west London rooftops and trees was outstanding, but the ambience of the room was rather heavy, as if everyone who had ever sat there to wait for an appointment – all the patients and their carers – had left something of their fear and sadness behind. The place smelled like a hospital, too. Stuffy and medicinal.

Marianne smiled, her brown eyes crinkling.

"You know what I mean, Faith!" she said. "Remember when you were eight and you sprained your ankle and we went to casualty? It was so gloomy in that little room where they put us to wait. All brown and dingy."

Faith smiled, too. She'd been terrified that day, and in quite a lot of pain. But Marianne had found a Travel Scrabble set in her handbag, and they'd set it up on the couch where Faith lay. They hadn't played the usual game. Marianne had invented a new one. *Make up your own word – and the more ridiculous the better!* By the time the orthopaedic consultant came to look at Faith's foot, the two of them were laughing hysterically. He'd even joined in, when they shared some of their zany brand-new words with him.

Marianne had always had this gift of bringing vitality and ease to an uncomfortable situation. It was impossible to think of her as unwell – as threatened by the insidious onset of Alzheimer's.

An elderly couple came into the waiting room and the husband helped his wife to sit on one of the chairs. He sat beside her, nodding a greeting to Faith and Marianne. His wife yawned capaciously and after a moment her eyes closed and she appeared to be dozing. She seemed completely unaware of her surroundings, and of the other people in the room. Faith tried not to think about it.

"Faith, lovey?" Marianne was touching her knee. "I've been meaning to ask you. How's Ben? Have you seen him at all?"

Faith looked sideways at her mother. Was it that obvious? Could her mother really read her so well?

"He's fine. We had coffee this morning, actually, before I picked you up from Ruth's."

Not wise, perhaps, to tell Marianne that the coffee had been drunk in the police station interview room, where Ben had just finished interrogating her as a suspect in a murder case.

The interview had gone smoothly – a much easier encounter than Faith had envisaged. Ben's manner had been crisp and professional, rather than harsh. He had pushed her to give him the details of her phone conversation with Sal, and to Faith's surprise there had been something quite healing in repeating the unpleasant words to him in the neutral setting of the interview room. Somehow, being put down on tape and filed away as evidence rendered them harmless.

Ben, of course, was not at all shocked by what Sal had said. He had far worse language hurled in his direction on a weekly basis. After he'd formally thanked her for her time, switched off the tape recorder, Faith said, "She was so inscrutable – what was it that was making her so upset that she swore at me?"

Ben shrugged. "Your guess is as good as mine, right now. Much food for thought."

He turned away and tapped a quick text message into his phone.

"All right?" he asked, looking up as he pocketed the phone. "Not too traumatic, being on the other side of the table?"

"No. I guess I got the 'good cop' treatment. Thanks."

He looked at her through his dark lashes. "Naturally, seeing as it's you."

This moment of lightness – of flirtation, almost – in the very formal situation, caught Faith off her guard, so that her head felt light and fluttery. *How am I supposed to respond to that?* She looked down at her hands, folded in her lap, and tried to get grounded again.

In a more serious tone, Ben added, "I think we can call the matter closed, Faith. It's clear that whatever expletives the woman chucked at you, her state of mind wasn't connected to your dealings with her. She had a bee in her bonnet, for sure, but we don't know what it was about. Not yet. I need to find out what she was doing – who she was with – on Sunday night. The analysis of the other calls on her mobile is pretty straightforward. She was in touch with her art dealer constantly. And there was one call to a solicitor. So… You're off the hook."

There was a tap on the door of the interview room and a fresh-faced young WPC came in with a tray from the canteen. Two bacon rolls, and two cups of frothy coffee – the result, no doubt, of the text Ben had just sent.

"Breakfast," he said. "As promised. Thanks, Jen."

Faith had forgotten the bacon butty that he'd mentioned when he left yesterday evening. She'd already had some breakfast – a bowl of muesli before leaving the vicarage – but the bacon roll smelled irresistibly delicious. The coffee was wonderful, too. Strong and bitter as she sipped it through the foamy milk.

"New cappuccino machine," Ben said. "Police canteen finally lumbering into the twenty-first century. What d'you think?"

"It's – lovely," Faith said, and she felt her face turning a little warm. Just the effect of the caffeine, that's all. Had to be.

Sitting beside her mother in the clinic waiting room, Faith's face felt warm again now. The expression in his eyes as he watched her drink that cup of coffee. Affectionate – intimate even – as he clocked her enjoyment.

Marianne leaned forward on her chair with a questioning look.

"Coffee? With Ben? This morning? There isn't something you're not telling me, is there, lovey?"

A door at the end of the waiting room clicked open. "Mrs Morgan?"

"That's us." Faith jumped up, relieved not to have to review the current state of her emotions with relation to her ex. What was it with Marianne, that she still seemed to consider him almost as one of the family?

"Oh dear," Marianne gave an uncharacteristic sigh as they walked across the waiting room. "Is it really necessary, all this? I know I forget things, sometimes, but doesn't everyone?" She touched Faith's arm. "I know you mean well, lovey – but sometimes I do think you and Ruth are overreacting."

"Maybe." Faith took her mother's hand and squeezed it.

Marianne could well be right. It was Ruth's nature to fret over things – to go looking for trouble before it found her. A little forgetfulness was no big deal. Even with the clipboard, Faith couldn't keep track of all her priorities. But – she must be loyal to her sister.

"Better safe than sorry, Mum," she whispered. 'We're just getting the full story, that's all. It's always good to have as much information as possible."

The consultant, Dr Malik, was a tall woman with glossy black hair knotted up on top of her head. She welcomed them into her sunny consulting room with an outstretched hand. After the introductions were over, the doctor opened up a folder in the centre of her desk.

"The consultant in Winchester has sent copies of your scans through," she said. "Along with his report."

"So what do you think?" Marianne asked, brightly. "Am I about to lose my marbles? I certainly don't feel as if I am."

"I know the scans show some early signs of… Alzheimer's," Faith added. "But my mother seems fine. She's living a very independent and busy life. It's just that occasionally she forgets things. I do, too. Perhaps it runs in the family!"

Dr Malik didn't respond to Faith's weak attempt at humour. She was quiet for a moment, and then she said, gently. "You're right about the scans. There are clear indications of Alzheimer's disease. These early signs can appear without any symptoms at all – in what we call the pre-clinical phase of the disease. But your consultant says that there is some mild cognitive impairment, too. And that your family felt it would be a good idea to get a second opinion on this."

Faith felt a sudden tightness in her throat. *The family. Just her and Ruth, now, to support Marianne. If only Dad were still here. He would be so upset, to think of Mum going through this on her own...*

Dr Malik was laying out what looked like a series of small, brightly coloured jigsaw puzzles on the desk in front of Marianne.

"Our research team here has developed some new cognitive tests," she said. "I thought you might like to have a go."

Marianne seemed to make light work of the puzzles. She had no problem naming the Prime Minister, either. Or putting together some short sentences that Dr Malik requested. Today's date, however, seemed to stump her.

"Thursday," she said, with confidence. "Thursday – the... something." Then she shook her head. "Sorry, it's just slipped my mind. Too much rushing about, this morning. It's all a bit... Ruth will know. She's..."

Marianne looked round and saw Faith in the chair beside her. "Oh. Is Ruth outside?" she asked. "Is she waiting for us?"

Faith's gut took a sudden swoop. A sensation somewhat similar to the feeling she'd had in the swish new lift, which had rushed them up here to the tenth floor of this hospital tower.

"No, Mum. I brought you today," she said, gently, holding her face neutral and relaxed. Marianne must on no account see any traces of panic. "We came on the train, remember? Ruth's in Winchester. At the council offices. She couldn't get off work."

"Oh goodness, yes." Marianne shook her head. "That's it. Silly me."

They were so sudden, so completely unexpected, these lapses. And so devastating, not just for Marianne. Faith thought back to last Christmas, to one awful moment when they were all together, celebrating at the vicarage, and her mother had turned to her and asked, her face bright with expectation, "Where's your father?"

"Don't worry," Dr Malik said, kindly. "Perhaps you can tell me what year it is?"

"1993," Marianne said, her eyes bright and confident.

"Not quite." Dr Malik shook her head.

Marianne's face melted into despair. Faith took her hand, and encouraged her to try again.

"Remember New Year's Eve, Mum? We were all at Ruth's, in Winchester. All together. Remember what the year was – that was just beginning? We drank champagne to celebrate."

"I'm sorry. I've no idea," Marianne said. "I'm feeling a bit – hot and bothered." Her hands, which had been resting in her lap, gripped each other in a sudden nervous gesture.

Dr Malik assured them it was no problem. She tidied away the puzzles.

Marianne had fallen silent. Her small frame seemed to have shrunk a little.

"How are we doing?" Faith asked Dr Malik.

"Not too bad at all. Just one point down on the score from her last test, in Winchester."

"I'm getting worse," Marianne murmured.

"It's nothing to worry about," Dr Malik said. "One point means really very little. And you may well be stressed and tired, after travelling all that way. It's a very hot day."

"What do we do now?" Faith asked, careful not to let her voice catch. "What – might we expect?"

"I'm afraid I can't be much help with the prognosis. There are no definite timeframes for the progression of the illness. It could be that Mrs Morgan—"

"Marianne!" Faith's mother chipped in. "You must call me Marianne. Everyone does."

Dr Malik smiled. "Of course. It could be, Marianne, that you remain relatively unimpaired for many years to come. That's the best-case scenario – and that's what we must hope for."

"And how do I ensure that I stay well?" Faith's mother braced her slight shoulders, sitting up tall again. "I must do everything I can."

"Mental stimulation is very important. Reading, doing puzzles – learning new skills. Exercise will help – in fact a general healthy, active lifestyle is the best way forward."

"No problem with that, then!" Faith said, a trickle of relief beginning to well up in her.

Dr Malik had just described Marianne's current lifestyle to a T. What with her love of reading the latest novels, her delight in trying new and complex recipes, her obsession with solving crosswords, and her passion for gardening, there was little more her mother could do. She loved to walk, too. Rarely a day passed that she wasn't out and about.

Marianne was already discussing all this with Dr Malik. Faith sat back in her chair and sent up a silent prayer of thanks for a sudden return of optimism. *Not the best news today –*

*but still much to hope for. And hope is the leaven that lifts any
difficulty into opportunity – into something positive and bright.
Thank you, Lord.*

After the consultation, Marianne wanted to take a stroll around
the neighbourhood. Faith was only too happy to comply. Her
mother seemed to have bounced back from her momentary
slump on hearing the doctor's diagnosis.

"I worked in this area when I was young, did you know?"
she was saying.

Marianne had stayed at home to look after Ruth and Faith
when they were small. It was hard to imagine her as a young
woman going out to work.

"I was a secretary for an architects' practice," she continued.
"Very interesting. So many obscure architectural terms I had
to know! *Architraves, axonometric projections,* and all sorts
of things I'd never heard of. The architects would record all
their letters and documents into a little machine, and I would
have to decode the results. Audio typing, that's what it was."
Marianne's face was glowing as she remembered. "And then,
of course, my lovey – there was this young site manager who
worked for the practice. He kept leaving things at the office so
he'd have to come back and pick them up. One day it was the
keys to the site, then next time it would be the plans…"

"Don't tell me," Faith interrupted. "It was Dad. And it was
really you he wanted to see."

Marianne's eyes were sparkling. "He was so shy he couldn't
bring himself to actually have a conversation with me. Only if
it was about some work thing."

"Dad? Shy?" Faith's heart gave a slight, painful shift. She
still missed him. His strong, calm certainty – the quiet wisdom

that had guided her through so many anxieties in her childhood and teenage years. "I'd never have thought of him like that."

Marianne hooked an arm through Faith's. "You didn't know him then," she said. "He was only twenty-two. Just a baby, really. And completely head-over-heels. We both were." Her voice was warm and affectionate as she continued: "You didn't know him till years later. People change. They grow up and mature. Being a father was wonderful for him. Gave him so much confidence. He was so proud of you both."

"And did you – stay in love with each other?" Faith felt surprisingly shy as she asked this. She had never questioned Marianne about her marriage before. "You certainly seemed as if you did."

Marianne showed no sign of embarrassment. "We were very happy together. Of course we had some ups and downs. In a long-term relationship you fall in and out of love over the years – the passion's there but it waxes and wanes. And you come in the end to something – how can I describe it? It might seem really quite ordinary – but it's wonderful. A closeness, a kindness, a sharing…"

Faith found herself thinking back to earlier that morning. To the moments when she and Ben sat at the table in the interview room, enjoying the bacon rolls together. There'd been something almost akin to what her mother was describing between them. A quietness, a shared moment of intimacy and acceptance.

Their relationship had been so stormy. Always so intense. But what if they had stayed together – if he'd tried to accept her vocation, and she'd had the patience – the charity, perhaps, was a better word – to accept his sharpness, his frequent intolerance. Might they have achieved something of what her mum had with her dad?

No chance for Faith to explore the feelings of regret that were trying to insinuate themselves into her consciousness. Marianne was tugging at her arm.

"There it is, lovey! Number 47! That's where the practice was. Where I met your father."

Faith looked across the street at a row of prosperous, well-kept shopfronts. Number 47 was a fish restaurant now, its door painted a fashionable duck-egg blue and an incongruous carved seagull on display in the window. All the tables looked to be full. "I wouldn't have recognized it, except for the number," Marianne commented. "This area has really come up in the world. The first time Dad asked me out, we went for a coffee. In those days, there was just one little Italian café, round the corner, where you could get espressos. We thought it was so sophisticated."

She fell silent and squeezed Faith's arm, urging her to walk on past. The complete transformation of the place that had been so important to her as a young woman seemed to have dampened her spirits a little.

After a few hundred yards, Faith looked up and saw a familiar street name. Lunn Place. Wasn't this where Sal's art dealer had his gallery? She steered her mother towards the turning.

"Would you like to see some paintings, Mum? By the artist who worked on the cover for our church booklet?" Faith had touched upon Sal's untimely death on the way up, deliberately avoiding the true horror of the murder.

"Why not?" said her mother.

Marianne and Faith walked along the pavement towards a gleaming plate-glass window with "Gallery" etched in large letters across it. Inside, Faith glimpsed several large canvases glowing with an intense reddish colour. She pushed open the door.

The gallery appeared to be empty. A chair and a desk stood by a door in the back wall, but there was no one about. Faith walked around, looking at the huge red paintings. They were of the Australian outback. Bare, thorny twigs broke through parched soil, and flocks of unfamiliar birds swirled darkly through pulsing, hot-yellow skies. In several of the paintings, a single human figure crouched under a rough shelter made of bark. It was impossible to tell whether the figure was an indigenous Australian, or someone of European origin. Faith felt an odd vibration – half fear, half excitement – as she stood to observe the scenes. With strong brushstrokes and a minimal palette of vibrant colour, Sal had captured the essence of the burning "red centre" of the vast continent. And there was a deep sense of aloneness, too. Of humanity pitted against the travails of existence.

"What do you think of this one?" Marianne's comment broke into Faith's meditation on the harsh landscapes.

Her mother was standing in front of a portrait of a tall male nude. He was young, probably not more than twenty or so. Pale-skinned and lean, there were taut muscles in his long limbs. His vivid blue eyes stared out from under his curly auburn hair with an imploring expression, a desperation or hunger.

"Ouch!" Faith couldn't help a little gasp of shock.

There was something tortured about the young man's expression, and the tension in his body. Yet he was beautiful, too; there was a wild sensuality in the sweeping brushstrokes that delineated his torso and limbs. If it hadn't been for that – the painting might almost have been a study for a crucifixion.

"Not very happy is he, poor lad?" Marianne said. "A troubled soul, I'd say."

"Like the artist," Faith said. "There she is."

A small self-portrait of Sal Hinkley hung next to the male nude. The artist's green eyes blazed out from the canvas. Her hair, redder in this likeness than Faith remembered it, had something of the vibrancy of the red earth in her landscapes.

"*She* took no prisoners, did she?" Marianne remarked.

"Good morning, ladies!" A well-spoken male voice echoed off the smooth walls. A man emerged from the door at the back.

"Outstanding, aren't they?" he boomed. "So – elemental. Typical of Hinkley's work. If you're looking to buy, you'll have to wait for the auction next Monday. Everything is in the sale. Have you seen the catalogue?"

Faith broke away from Sal's challenging gaze. Patrick Mills was much as she'd imagined him – tall, slightly swelling around the middle but carrying the bulk well. Greying but with a thick head of hair. The only thing she hasn't reckoned on was the bristling dark moustache. His loud, hearty tone set Faith slightly on edge. Why was he making no mention of Sal's so very recent death?

"I don't want to buy a painting," said Faith. "We were passing, and I really wanted my mother to see Sal's work. The artist was a remarkable woman. Her death is a great loss."

Patrick Mills gave a little start. "Ah," he managed to say.

"Did you know her well?" Faith asked.

"I'm sorry. Are you – Press?" Mills's bushy eyebrows pulled down low over his hooded eyes. "You'll have to make an appointment. I'm not giving any unscheduled interviews."

Faith explained who she was. "We spoke on the telephone, do you remember? The day after Sal died."

"Of course!" Mills grasped her hand. His palm felt clammy against hers. "I'm awfully sorry. There's been a pesky journalist sniffing around these last couple of days. I thought you must be another of 'em."

Faith extracted her hand from his. "I'm a little surprised that the auction is going ahead. So soon after—"

"It's what Sal would have wanted," Mills interrupted. "She wasn't one for sentiment. Here – take a look at the catalogue." He thrust a large, glossy brochure into Faith's hands.

Faith found herself taking it, but couldn't arrange her features into a smile. There was something deeply unsavoury about the way that Patrick Mills was using Sal's unconventional personality to excuse the fact that he'd decided not to cancel the sale. She supposed he stood to earn a hefty commission.

A phone rang from the desk. The art dealer bustled over to answer it. Faith opened the catalogue. Inside was a printed sheet of A4 paper, entitled "Obituary".

There was a brief statement about the artist's work, beginning: *Sal Hinkley's uncompromising spirit led her to some of Australia's bleakest and most challenging wildernesses. Here she found a timeless landscape in which the transience of human existence was bleakly laid bare. This became a keynote of the artist's work.*

The slick, commercial nature of this type of "artspeak" wouldn't normally have appealed to Faith. But today, she felt herself resonate with what she had just read. *The transience of existence.* She was reminded once more of the ever-flowing tide of humanity that had passed through St James's – of the struggle to survive that most parishioners would have endured in the past. *For most human beings, life is short. It is bleak and tough,* she thought. *We are so protected from the realities in the comforts of our Western, twenty-first-century lifestyles...*

At the bottom of the page, a short paragraph printed in red ink had been added: *Those intending to bid at the upcoming Auction should please note that due to the posthumous nature of the sale, guide prices may be subject to a considerable increase.*

Faith felt slightly sick. How ghoulishly inappropriate. She tucked the piece of paper back inside the catalogue and asked her mother if she was ready to leave.

"I am if you are," Marianne replied. "It must be almost lunchtime. I could murder a nice baguette. Ham and cheese. Shall we see if we can find one?"

CHAPTER

9

On the train back to Winchester, Faith allowed herself to do nothing. Marianne, ensconced in the seat opposite, was a very undemanding companion. She was happily engrossed with the crossword in the free newspaper she'd picked up on the Underground. Faith lolled back in her seat and watched the sun-baked countryside flash past. It had been an emotional day, in more ways than one, and it would do her good to enjoy a little downtime to process it all. The clipboard was waiting for her at the vicarage, and there wasn't much she could do without it. Two missed calls had just come through on her mobile, one from Bella Wythenshaw and one from George Casey. But there was no point in trying to speak to them. It wasn't worth the frustration. She'd only get cut off due to the intermittent signal along the route of the railway.

Their train had just left Basingstoke, and was well into the last leg of the journey when Marianne filled in the last clue and folded up the paper.

"Faith?" She leaned forward in her seat.

"Mum?" Faith recalled her attention from the fields and the trees – a landscape that even in this heatwave seemed almost tropically lush, compared with the stark Australian vistas in Sal's paintings.

Marianne's expression was unusually serious. She laid a gentle hand on Faith's knee. "My mother had dementia, you know. It came on very early. She was only fifty-seven."

"What?" Faith straightened up, trying to disguise how shocked she was. "You never told us."

"Oh, you were much too small," said her mother. "And we didn't really dwell on that sort of thing. We didn't make a fuss." Marianne's eyes were distant. "We just – got on with it. At first Mother was a bit forgetful, so we looked out for her. At least, my sisters did most of it. I had you and Ruth to care for, so I could only do so much. And then…" She hesitated.

"Then what?" Faith tried to speak gently.

"Well. It's a long story, lovey. And not a very happy one. In the end Mother didn't even know who we were. She lost her speech – and all her dignity. She didn't even care about keeping herself clean. It was so sad."

Pity surged in Faith for her grandmother, for the old woman she had barely known – just glimpsed on occasions, prowling around her home in a dressing gown, with a rather cross expression on her wrinkled face – and also for the young mother that Marianne had been.

"Mum – I wish you'd spoken about this," she said. "Shared it with us."

"You were much too young, my darling. You wouldn't have understood and you would have been upset."

"Oh, Mum." The train rattled under a bridge, and for a second the sunlight was blocked out.

"We were very lucky," Marianne said, reaching across to take Faith's hand. "Dr Gowan – do you remember him?"

"Vaguely," Faith said, picturing a white moustache and black-rimmed glasses. "He came when we had measles. And brought us boiled sweets."

"That's him!" Marianne smiled. "A lovely man. He was very good to Mother at the end." She lowered her voice, but the carriage was almost empty. "There was nothing he could do to make her better. But he – helped."

Her brown eyes were very grave as they looked into Faith's. "You mean he…?"

Her mother nodded.

Faith frowned, unsure of how to process the information, confronted head-on with a debate which had always seemed rather remote and rhetorical. She knew, of course, that it was hardly a rare occurrence, especially if one went back a couple of generations, but the idea of the kindly doctor from her childhood taking part in such an act made her distinctly uneasy. It cast dark clouds over her memories. She leaned her head back against the seat and watched the fields pass by. It was illegal, of course, in the bluntest sense, however dire the suffering of the patient. She had seen, and continued to see, elderly people in rather terrible states in her work at the local hospices. Those quiet, peaceful places where kindly nurses shepherded the residents through their final days. Perhaps some wanted to die, but just as many seemed to find a serenity in their final hours on earth – a joy, even. The doctor's needle and the sudden rush of killing chemicals seemed such a blunt instrument in comparison.

The pressure of her mother's fingers, warm and gentle, brought Faith back to the present, to the two of them, leaning so close together in the hot railway carriage. *There is only now. We must live in the now.*

"We never spoke of it, lovey," said Marianne. "But he was very good to her. I hope I'll be as lucky, when my time comes. I hope there'll be someone to help me. I don't want to suffer like that. Or to be a burden to Ruth and you…"

Faith realized what her mother was driving at, and it threw her into confusion. "You'll never be a burden," she said. She reached to hug her mother, holding her very tight, hoping that her mother would say no more. And so tight that Marianne wouldn't be able to see the tears that had sprung up in her daughter's eyes. "And anyway – remember what Dr Malik said. You've got many, many years of happy and active life to come."

At the station, they picked up Faith's car and drove back to Ruth's little house. The clipboard was flapping wildly in the forefront of Faith's mind, but she was reluctant to leave her mother alone.

"Would you like me to come in and keep you company for a while? I could make you a sandwich."

Marianne's ham-and-cheese baguette had proved elusive. Their route from the gallery to the Underground station was lined with fine-dining outlets, not sandwich shops and take-outs, and by the time they reached Waterloo there was only the opportunity to grab a cup of tea and a scone from one of the coffee kiosks. That was a while ago now. And the scones had been rather dry and disappointing.

Marianne glanced at her watch. "Goodness, no. Thanks for the offer but I've got badminton in forty-five minutes. I've booked a session at the sports centre with Peggy Milton. Brian's aunt, remember? And some of her friends. They play twice a week. I'll see you soon. And thank you for everything today."

"Badminton? I didn't know you played." Faith hadn't noticed any reserve in her mother's manner as she mentioned Brian. Could it be that she had just accepted his return, without question? *Is it only me that thinks Ruth is moving too fast – that she should be more careful?* A worse thought occurred – that her mum's calm demeanour was due to her decreasing mental faculty. She surely hadn't forgotten Brian's two decades of absence?

"Yes, lovey. Just once a week – but it's very good for keeping me flexible." Marianne smiled and rolled her shoulders back to demonstrate. "And good for the heart, too, of course. A cardiovascular workout."

Faith wanted to hug her mother again, but Marianne was already hurrying off, saying she must organize her kit and get changed or she would be late.

"Goodbye, Mum. Enjoy your game."

Be glad she's so active and so independent still, she told herself. *And you have plenty of other commitments to worry about.* She got out her mobile and checked in to the first voicemail message.

"Faith – it's Bella. I'm so sorry to ring you like this – it's just…" There was a pause as Bella's breath caught in a sob. She sounded extremely distressed. *"The police – they came back today. To – talk to us. And Daniel! It was so awful. I don't know why I'm calling you. I suppose because – Inspector Shorter… he's a friend of yours, isn't he? – he was just so – oh dear… I'm sorry… it doesn't matter."*

The message ended.

Anger surged in Faith and she found herself clutching the phone so tightly she was surprised it didn't crack apart in her hand. *Ben!* He might have received the information that

Sal had been absent from the B&B on Sunday night with a certain aplomb, but of course he had gone straight round to the Wythenshaw's to interrogate them again. With his usual complete disregard for anything except cutting through to the truth.

She'd had to tell him. It was an important piece of evidence. But... *Oh, Ben.*

The next message kicked in.

"Good afternoon, Faith. I trust you are having a good day." George Casey's clipped, officious voice.

"Not particularly," Faith said, curtly, to the voicemail.

He'd probably found out about the dent in her car – and possibly also the fact that, briefly, she'd been a suspect in the murder. George had worked as a Religious Affairs correspondent for one of the national newspapers before he became the diocesan press officer, and while in that role he'd acquired a bloodhound's nose for any whiff of scandal around him. He wouldn't be at all happy to hear the incumbent of St James's had been interviewed at police headquarters.

She waited, expecting to hear George's inevitable request to keep all details of the prang and her subsequent interview with Ben absolutely undercover, so that St James's was in no way implicated. Instead, he simply said: *"Could you give me a call, when you've got a moment? Nothing urgent."*

He didn't sound at all perturbed. Unlikely, then, that he knew about her visit to the police headquarters. Well – if what he wanted to discuss wasn't urgent, it could wait. Faith's energy was quite depleted after the trip to London, and she still had so much to do. She stopped off at a petrol station to pick up a coffee and a muffin, and headed out to the Wythenshaw's B&B by the River Itchen.

This time, Daniel didn't come rushing to greet Faith with a hug. He had gone to ground in the lounge, where he was sitting on the hearthrug, hugging his knees and looking down into the empty grate.

"What happened?" Faith asked his mother. "I've never seen him withdrawn like that. Is he all right?"

Bella shepherded her through into the kitchen. "I hope so. He won't say a word. Hasn't spoken to us once since Inspector Shorter left. He's so upset."

Bella's eyes were red and she looked completely drained.

Faith pictured, with a sinking feeling, exactly what had happened during Daniel's interrogation with Ben, and Bella confirmed her suspicions.

"The inspector kept asking him about Sal Hinkley. Daniel, of course, said he didn't like her. And that was it. The questions just kept on coming: *Why were you angry with her? Did you want to hurt her? No wonder she didn't want to spend another night here.*"

"I can imagine," Faith said. *Ben, badgering the frightened young man without any thought as to the aftermath.* "It must have been incredibly distressing for all of you." She took the kettle to the sink and filled it. Bella looked like she could do with a cup of tea.

"I presume you were present at the interview? As Daniel's 'responsible adult'?"

Bella nodded. "I'm glad it was me and not Gavin. I think he'd have punched the inspector. There was a policewoman, too, sitting there listening. But she didn't have much to say for herself. I tried to explain that Daniel was vulnerable."

So a chaperone had been present. She would have been there to intervene, if she felt that there was anything inappropriate in the way that Ben handled the interview. Yet perhaps, like so many of the younger officers, she found Detective Inspector Shorter a little intimidating. It was a difficult situation, and Faith found herself apologizing on behalf of the force. She was wholeheartedly with Bella regarding the way Daniel had been treated.

"Daniel was so confused," Bella said. "He really had no idea what was going on. He just kept saying that he hated Sal, that she was a bad person for shouting at me. The inspector kept harping on and on at him. Then – and this was the worst – he said they had to get a DNA swab. Can you imagine? The poor lamb was already terrified, and there they were, trying to poke things into his mouth. He started yelling and shouting and trying to lash out at the inspector. You can imagine how that looked."

Bella sat down at the kitchen table. She made no comment as Faith found a box of tea bags and some mugs. She'd never normally have allowed anyone to make tea in her kitchen, but all the willpower and energy seemed to have drained away from her.

As she allocated a tea bag to each mug, Faith thought back to the morning following Sal's death. Something was niggling at the back of her mind. Hadn't Fred said something about Daniel? That he'd been expecting him to help with the digging on Tuesday morning, but the lad hadn't turned up? That can't be relevant, she told herself. Sal died the night before.

Bella started up again. "To cap it all, Inspector Shorter wouldn't even say why he was suspicious of Daniel. I suppose one of our guests – someone who saw him get upset when Sal and I were arguing – must have gone to the police."

"Possibly." Faith found a packet of biscuits in one of the cupboards and spilled half a dozen out onto a plate. The kettle was hissing already, a trickle of steam issuing from its spout.

"And you know what?" Bella said, with uncharacteristic venom. "It was all for nothing, all that questioning. They've ruled him out of their enquiries, because he couldn't possibly have done it. We never allow him to leave the house without one of us accompanying him."

"Were you both at home that night? You and Gavin?" Faith poured hot water into mugs.

"No!" Bella said, with a sigh. "Just Gavin was here. It was Monday – our evening to do the supermarket shop. All three of us usually go, and Daniel helps out with loading the car. But Gavin said he wasn't feeling too great. He wanted to stay at home. Daniel stayed with him. There was some cartoon thing he wanted to watch on TV. So – lucky me – I had to do that mammoth shop for the B&B all on my own. Mind you, they are good at the supermarket. Really helpful. One of the young lads who organizes the trolleys helped me pack the car."

Faith put a couple of spoons of sugar into a mug of tea and passed it to Bella.

"Oh, that's nice," Bella said, sipping it. "I don't usually have sugar. But – sometimes it's just – right. Just what you want."

"It's good for shock. And you've had a very rough time," Faith said. She offered to take some tea to Daniel, and Bella said that might be a good idea, though she couldn't guarantee that he would speak to Faith.

The young man was still on the floor. When Faith put the digestives in front of him, he looked round at her, his face a picture of misery.

"I'm a bad boy," he said. "The man said."

Faith squatted down beside him, careful not to let him see how angry she was. Ben could show care and empathy when he wanted to. He had been so careful, so sensitive with her in the interview room that morning. Why not with this very vulnerable young man? That callousness in Ben, the ruthless no-holds-barred approach he used in pursuit of a confession was the one thing that had really broken the bond between them. It was something she could never tolerate. All human beings deserved respect and consideration, whatever they might be suspected of. But Ben had always insisted the hard-man act was just that – an act, a piece of theatre, a strategy. He'd said on more than one occasion that she lacked the killer instinct needed to be a detective. *You have to play dirty, Fay, because the world's a dirty place.* Perhaps he was right, in some respects. And that was why she'd begun to suspect the police force wasn't for her.

"I think you're a good boy, Daniel," she said. "And I also think you should eat these nice biscuits. And then you can go and help Mum wash up the tea mugs. How about that?"

"All right, Faith," Daniel replied, and a shadowy smile emerged on his face.

Driving back to Little Worthy half an hour or so later, Faith was troubled and felt ashamed for it. Bella had told her that Gavin wanted to stay at home with his son on Monday night, but that raised other questions and she would be surprised if Ben wasn't thinking the same. For it was just conceivable that Gavin could have left Daniel in front of the TV and headed over to Sal's hut without his son even noticing he had gone out.

Faith slowed behind a truck. What if he'd gone to remonstrate with the artist for her bad behaviour towards his wife and to ask her – privately, away from the B&B and the other guests – not to be so rude in future? And perhaps Sal had sworn at him, and things had got out of control. It wasn't hard to imagine Gavin getting angry, especially if his family were concerned.

Faith's mind was locking in to deductive mode, running swiftly through the possibilities.

Faith shook the thoughts away. It was natural to speculate, of course, but these people were first and foremost her parishioners, not her suspects. That she was tired and hungry didn't help.

The only thing in the vicarage fridge was a ready meal of macaroni cheese and some wilting lettuce leaves. To her annoyance, Faith found herself thinking of those bacon rolls in the interview room.

Get out of my mind, Ben. She shoved the macaroni cheese into the microwave and turned it on. Time to locate the clipboard. She could flip through it and do some prioritizing for tomorrow while she ate.

CHAPTER

10

On Friday morning, a harsh clatter from the direction of Shoesmith's Farm woke Faith at seven-thirty. It sounded as if the builders had abandoned the chainsaw and were attacking the old farmhouse in a more radical way, with a pneumatic drill. They must have started early to avoid the worst of the heat.

Thank goodness it was Saturday tomorrow. Presumably Jeremy would give them the weekend off. Though perhaps she should be grateful for the racket – or she might just have slept on through.

She yawned deeply and rolled over in the big bed. If it hadn't been for the great multitude of tasks to be completed before Sunday, she might have hugged a pillow to her ear and grabbed a few moments more sleep. But in all honesty, she should really have been up and running at least an hour ago if she was going to get everything done.

Over a mug of instant coffee and a slice of toast, Faith sat down with her laptop and caught up with some urgent emails before heading over to the church.

The porch was awash with a sea of large cardboard boxes. Fred was standing over one of them, which he'd torn open. He looked round, his red face beaming with pleasure.

"Look – our booklets!" he said. "I couldn't wait. Had to have a gander."

He held one up for Faith to see. As per Pat's instructions, on the front of the booklet a black-and-white photograph of the Green in 1900 had been cleverly spliced with a contemporary colour image from this year.

"Look at that, eh? Not much has changed," Fred said. "Not outwardly, anyway."

Faith helped herself to a booklet and leafed through it to check that everything had been included.

Elsie Lively – one of the oldest members of Faith's congregation and for many years the village postmistress – had contributed a double-page spread on her family history, running back eight generations to the late 1700s. The succession of births, marriages and deaths could be found laid out more starkly in the parish records – and also in the moss-covered inscriptions in the churchyard.

Among the illustrations, the Cartwrights' photo of the old forge had been beautifully reproduced. There was a snapshot of Gwen Summerly's cottage, too, in the 1950s, when it appeared to have been a shop. A tin sign nailed above the door to the shop advised: "Nightly Bile Beans Keep You Slim, Healthy and Active."

"My mother used to get our groceries from that shop, after the war," Fred said, looking over Faith's shoulder. "I was just a little 'un then. The old girl that ran it made toffee in the back kitchen. Big sheets of it. Hard as marble, it was. She'd break it into pieces for us with a hammer. When she died they bricked up the shop window and turned it into a dwelling. All we had left then was the post office."

Presumably the Bile Beans were some kind of early twentieth-century over-the-counter remedy for constipation. Faith refrained from asking Fred if he'd ever tried them.

On the next page, a map of Little Worthy in the 1930s showed the Green and its cottages surrounded by wide acres of farmland. Most of these fields no longer existed. They'd disappeared under the council houses and the newer private estates that now formed the bulk of the village. Faith remarked on this.

"That's right." Fred nodded. "Shoesmith's Farm was the biggest for miles around until they sold off the land in '53."

And now it was changing yet again, Faith thought, listening to the remorseless rattle of the drill. Jeremy Taylor was remodelling the ancient farmhouse and barns into a luxury twenty-first-century rural retreat. Whatever would the labourers who had toiled on the land over the centuries, trudging through mud to make a meagre living, make of Jeremy's Jacuzzi and his ultra-modern kitchen with all its hi-tech gadgets?

"I've got to say, though," Fred began, with a shy glance at Faith, "your foreword, that's my favourite part. I couldn't put it down."

"Why – thank you, Fred!" Faith was touched to see the genuine emotion on his face.

"All those miles, from France to Santiago. I never thought of you as a walker."

"I'm not, really," Faith said. "I never seem to have the time. But I had to do the pilgrimage. I knew I wanted to be part of the church, but I didn't know how. I couldn't see the path ahead of me. I thought the walk to Santiago might help."

"Very fitting, how you've pulled it all together – Sant Iago, St James – just the thing for the Saint's Day celebrations."

"That's very kind of you, Fred."

Faith closed the booklet, and – saving the best for last – she turned it over to look at the back cover.

"What?" she gasped, unable to believe her eyes.

The reproduction that confronted her wasn't Sal's bold depiction of the north face of the church with the storm clouds behind it. Instead, a demure, soft-focus watercolour of the south face had been substituted. The sky above the chocolate-box rendition of St James's was a misty lavender blue, and a pastel rainbow of spring flowers sprouted between the graves in the churchyard. The church's ancient stone walls had been given a sugary, soft-focus quality. *It might as well be a gingerbread house!* Faith thought, her heart racing as the full charge of anger hit her. Then she understood what she was looking at. Someone had substituted one of Gwen Summerly's watercolours for Sal's oil painting!

Making her excuses to Fred, she ran into the vestry and picked up the phone to call the printer. He seemed perturbed by her slightly shrill tone.

"I'm sorry, vicar," he said. "But one of your church councillors called yesterday afternoon, just before we went to press. He told us there'd been a last-minute change with regards to the back cover. We weren't to use the painting you brought over. He came by with the new image."

"Really?" Faith struggled to keep her voice calm. "So someone from the Parochial Church Council called you. And who might that have been?"

"It was a Mr Taylor, if I remember rightly," the printer

said. "I assumed we should go ahead with what he said. He was quite clear that's what the council wanted."

"Right. Thank you." Faith terminated the call. Her head was in turmoil. Something very fishy was going on, even something distinctly underhand. It had been such a close-run thing, the council vote for the commission. But even though just one vote had tipped the balance in Sal's favour when it came to the final show of hands – it was still a majority. How could Jeremy Taylor see fit to overrule that? It was a privilege for St James's to have the work of such a renowned and gifted artist for a nominal fee. And now it had been thrown away – cancelled out by a devious, small-minded act of betrayal. Faith looked down. She was so angry that her hands were shaking.

The vestry door creaked. Pat Montague was standing on the threshold, watching Faith warily. Faith took a deep breath to compose herself.

"Pat, can you explain to me the meaning of this?" Faith strove to keep her voice steady. She held up the booklet.

"Oh dear," Pat blustered, her cheeks very pink. "I knew you wouldn't be happy about it. But Jeremy and I talked it through. We really couldn't go along with the council's choice."

"What on earth do you mean?"

Pat's eyes darted around the vestry, looking everywhere but at Faith. 'The Hinkley woman's painting was not apprrropriate at all, in our view. Jeremy had a word with George Casey, and George said he was right behind us, if we weren't happy and we wanted to change it. So – we went ahead."

"I see," said Faith coldly.

She thought back to the day that Sal's body had been found. Jeremy and George had been sitting together in the church, talking intently. Maybe they were plotting this little act of insurrection even then. Pat was still hovering in the door, looking extremely uncomfortable. It wasn't fair to heap all the blame on her head – she had some powerful co-conspirators.

"I suppose that what's done is done, though I find this very hard to come to terms with," Faith said. "You made it very clear that you didn't like Sal's work – but she won the vote, Pat. And you went behind my back and changed the decision. I can't help but think that you and Jeremy have been underhand. Devious, even."

Strong words, but Faith had no desire to moderate them. She put the booklet down on the table in the vestry and walked out. Pat made no attempt to follow her. For once, the voluble churchwarden had nothing to say.

Outside in the churchyard, the sun was picking up strength. Faith stepped into the shade of one of the yew trees and pulled out her mobile. George Casey picked up on her first ring. She launched in without giving him the opportunity to speak.

"George? I do not appreciate being kept in the dark if you see fit to overturn a democratic decision of our church council. There's absolutely no justification for such duplicitous behaviour."

"You have hold of the wrong end of the stick, Faith." George seemed completely unruffled by her words. His tone was unctuous. "I called you yesterday, when all this came to a head. I left a message. Didn't you get it?"

Faith slapped her forehead. *Of course!* The "non-urgent" message that she hadn't seen fit to respond to! How could she have let that slip by? A moment of clarity stilled her racing thoughts. *Wait a moment. Surely the printers would have taken most of yesterday to run off all those boxes of booklets.*

"George, when you left that message, you gave me no hint as to what it was you wanted to speak to me about. And it was past lunchtime when you rang. It occurs to me that what you were actually doing was presenting me with a *fait accompli.* What time did the booklet go to press? In the morning, surely, with such a high volume to be printed."

George Casey didn't deign to answer this. "The key issue here," he said, "is the death of the artist. We all felt it would be insensitive – a little macabre, even – to feature the work of someone so recently deceased in suspicious circumstances on the cover of a booklet intended to celebrate the history of our church."

"And it didn't occur to you that to honour her work might have been a fitting memorial?" Faith's anger was building again.

Once again, George pressed on with his own agenda. "You have to admit – the picture was perhaps a little gloomy. *Dark*, one might even say."

Faith took a long breath, trying to formulate the words that would convey to George her admiration for the painting – her conviction that it was right, sometimes, to show the storm clouds…

"Anyway," George interjected, a note of triumph creeping into his voice. "I should have thought, what with your rather unfortunate connection to the artist…"

"I beg your pardon? What connection? I admired her work, but I barely knew Sal Hinkley."

"Oh, I think you know what I'm talking about," he continued. "And let me tell you, I've had to expend a considerable amount of energy keeping this sordid business out of the papers." George's tone was impossibly smug.

So – his ex-Fleet Street instincts had led him to uncover the unfortunate prang on Monday morning – and the altercation with Sal, too, presumably. How utterly infuriating that he should now try to use this against her. What was the use of trying to make a point when he simply wrong-footed her at every turn?

"The whole affair looks distinctly dodgy. Why didn't you come clean about it?" George's voice was strident, gathering volume as he continued. "Why haven't you brought everything out into the open and pursued an insurance claim, as any right-minded person would do? The conclusion one must come to is that you had some secret *connection* with the artist, which you wished to keep quiet about. And as to the nature of that connection – well, I don't care to speculate."

Faith took a deep breath. She had to stop this. "George. Congratulations. I hope you're very pleased. Have a good day."

As she hung up, she almost flung her mobile across the churchyard. Only the sight of a tall figure striding through the gravestones towards her stopped her from doing this. Ben. Faith bit her lip. Trust him to show up at the worst possible moment.

"Hello, Fay." He joined her under the tree. A small smile appeared on his lips as he noted her expression. "That was all rather heated. Couldn't help overhearing. Anything you'd like to share with me?"

Faith counted to five before speaking. He knew how rattled she was – he could always pick up on her mood. Best to stay as calm as she could.

"Yes, actually. I have a bone to pick with you. I think someone in your department's been gossiping about the dent in my car. And my argument with Sal."

Ben shrugged. "Is it such a big deal?"

"Absolutely. I've just been talking to the press officer for the diocese. He's always horrified at any little irregularity that might reflect badly on the church. Especially where I'm concerned. You could have asked your colleagues to be discreet about this, Ben."

"Sorry." Ben seemed genuinely contrite.

Faith pocketed her phone.

"I heard something about a booklet?" Ben said hopefully.

Sniffing around on the trail again. Yet he wasn't being pushy. He was just asking. Faith felt her anger trickle away, losing itself in the dry, packed soil beneath her feet.

She told Ben about the substitution of Gwen's watercolour. "It's just a church wrangle, that's all. The old guard trying to keep anything new and a bit controversial at bay. And using rather iffy methods to do so."

Ben's eyebrows lifted, an infinitesimal but unmistakeable movement. Something in her words had caught his attention.

"Tell me more," he said.

"It's nothing, Ben. Just a bit of PCC politics. The diehards going behind my back to avoid a confrontation. That's all."

A familiar steely glint came into Ben's blue eyes. He was not going to back down.

"Give me the full story," he said. "Everything."

Faith kept her tone light as she explained about Sal's narrow victory in the council vote. "Sal's painting really wasn't Pat and Jeremy's cup of tea. I suppose they felt that she'd won by such a small margin it wouldn't matter if they overturned the decision. And George – the press officer – was willing to back them up. He didn't like the painting, either."

"Well." The little smile was widening. "Curious, eh?"

Faith felt suddenly uneasy. Ben had already interviewed Pat, Jeremy and George. Surely they weren't still on the list of suspects? Not over something that amounted, when all was said and done, to a simple matter of taste.

"Ben. Don't go there. It was just a bit of a squabble, honestly. You're barking up the wrong tree."

Ben ignored this. "So who voted for the watercolour you didn't like? Did this Casey fellow vote for it?" His tone had shifted. Still friendly, but more forceful.

"He abstained, if I remember rightly," said Faith. "Ben – it's really not worth pursuing this."

He grinned then, a quick flash of white teeth. "I'll be the judge of that."

Faith's bare forearms prickled with irritation. She remembered the conversation with Bella, yesterday, about Ben's rough handling of Daniel. And here he was, once again picking up the scent of something suspicious, and tracking it remorselessly. The end justifying the means every time. Should she take him to task for the way that he handled the interview with Daniel? Was it even worth it?

"Hey, how about this," Ben spoke in a softer tone, looking at her sideways. "You dish me the dirt on your church council and I tell you the latest on the murder weapon. Deal?"

"Ben…"

"Oh, come on, Fay," he said. "Don't pretend you aren't interested."

He'd obviously noticed her irritation and he'd dropped his aggressive tone. He was playing her, though. She was wise enough to know that.

"No way," Faith said. In spite of herself, her face was softening into a smile. She forced herself to look away.

"So, if Casey didn't vote for Hinkley's painting, who did?" Ben asked.

"I can't remember. It's in the PCC minutes, if you really want to know."

"Ah, the blessed minutiae of church record-keeping. Where would we be without it? What did you sell at the last church fete? I bet it's all there, right down to the last brick of a rock cake."

Faith looked at Ben again. "It's not working."

Ben shrugged and stared across the churchyard for a few seconds.

"They say Sal was strangled with a piece of thin cord," he said at last. "Thin-ish, anyway. A woman's belt, possibly."

Faith glanced at him, surprised.

"Yup. A woman's belt. Might have been Ms Summerly's, perhaps? Your wishy-washy watercolour painter?"

"Gwen's a middle-aged lady, Ben. She would never have the strength to kill someone with a belt."

Ben chuckled. "Ah, but she might have had a friend. A lady accomplice. *Many hands make light work.* What about your old Pat? I wouldn't fancy going head to head with that one…"

"Don't, Ben. Stop it. That's going too far." Faith took a step back from him. "It's not on. Pat's my churchwarden."

"Hey, take it easy." Ben's face darkened. "Where's your sense of humour, Fay? You'd have gone with it, once. We all used to take the mickey out of each other all the time. Remember? All in good fun."

"I don't see it like that. Not any more. This is a very different situation and it's not on."

She half-expected him to turn his back on her, but he

didn't. He stood under the yew tree, leaning one hand up against the trunk.

"I was going to make you an offer," he said, in a resigned, almost sad tone. "But I'm pretty sure I know what the response will be."

"Why ask, then?" she asked.

"I thought you might like to have dinner tomorrow. Over at my new flat. You've never seen it. Would you come?"

"No," Faith said, quickly, shocked at the swift reaction in her body. The sudden loosening of her limbs at the thought of being with him again; just the two of them, alone in a domestic environment. "I don't think it's wise. Do you?"

"Why not?" Ben stared down at the cracked, dry earth under the tree. "Early dinner. I cook, you take a snoop round the flat. That's all."

"Oh, Ben."

"Is that a 'yes', then?"

Faith thought of last night's soggy microwaved macaroni cheese. And she would barely have time to get to the shops today to replenish the fridge.

"I'm absolutely overwhelmed with work," she said. "The anniversary's the day after tomorrow. I'm rushed off my feet."

"I know you are. That's why I'm cooking dinner for you. Six?"

She didn't have the will to fight. "OK. But I can't stay long."

He slapped the tree trunk and headed off towards the lychgate, a slight jauntiness in his step.

Faith stayed where she was. She took a long slow breath, trying to release the tangled emotions that possessed her. Of which her pent-up rage over the booklet was still by far the strongest. She'd been lied to by those that she should be able to trust implicitly. But it was done now. There was nothing she could do to reinstate Sal's painting. Best to move on. The clipboard was waiting for her in the vestry. And, God willing, there was still most of the long summer's day to work through those clamouring Post-it notes.

CHAPTER

11

On Saturday morning, Faith stumbled downstairs at seven o'clock to discover a handwritten note on the doormat. It was from Fred. *My girls are working overtime this week – please use the results!* She unlocked the front door and picked up the box of half a dozen eggs he had left for her on the doorstep. Fred kept a few hens on his allotment, and when he didn't manage to sell all the eggs, he'd offer them to Faith. The eggs were always fresh, and – just as this morning – were usually accompanied in their box by the soft curl of a brown feather.

Faith went out into the garden and snipped some chives, parsley and thyme from the border by the garden wall. The bricks of the wall had cooled down overnight, but the air in the garden already felt quite warm. Luckily, the herbs hadn't suffered too much from the July heat and the lack of rain. Alas, the same could not be said for the flowering annuals that Fred had planted out for her back in May. Some of them were still just about alive, though their heads were hanging, but many had wilted away to nothing. Faith was about to go and find the watering can when she remembered her father's advice, from childhood days. *Never water a plant in sunshine, or you'll scorch the leaves.*

She went inside to make breakfast, a fluffy hillock of scrambled eggs topped with fresh green herbs. It was delicious, though somewhat spoiled by the fact that she decided to open up her laptop and skim through a few of the emails while she ate. At the top of the inbox was a message from Ruth, sent just a few minutes before. She must have written it as soon as she got up. *Hi Faith. Thanks so much for taking Mother to London; she really enjoyed spending some time with you at last.* Hard to tell, from those typed words, whether Faith's sister was being ironic. Whether she intended a sly dig at Faith, with that *at last.* Emails were so bland, they simply didn't give the subtle nuances of communication. Faith read on: *She's staying down a few more days, says she wants to come to your "do" tomorrow, so we'll bring her along. I'm worried about her, Faith. I really think she needs to be nearer to us, just in case she suddenly deteriorates. I'm sure you'll agree this is a good idea. Just a question of persuading her that she must leave the house in Birmingham. I doubt it will be easy. Anyway. Thanks again. Let's talk soon. Big Sis x*

Maybe Ruth's thanks were genuine, with no sting in the tail. "Big Sis" was an old joke of theirs. Ruth was the elder sister by four years, but she was two inches shorter, and had been so ever since Faith went through a growth spurt at the age of thirteen. Ruth was slimmer, too. Slighter in every way, Faith thought with a sigh, as she pushed the plate of half-finished scrambled eggs away.

She abandoned the email inbox and moved to the Internet search option, typing in *long term prognosis for Alzheimer's.*

It was impossible to read through the words that came

up on the screen without feeling a leaden, numbing weight of apprehension at what might lie in store for her mother.

Personality change. Faith remembered the woman in the dementia clinic waiting room, lost in her own sleepy little world. In a few years' time the lively and sociable Marianne might show the same bored indifference to whatever was going on around her. *Loss of language.* What an absolute hell not to be able to communicate: to share the joy of life with others, or to tell them if things were not good with you, if you needed something. No wonder that *Episodes of Irritability* was also listed. *Inability to recognize family and friends.* No chance to thank those who cared for you. Not even with the squeeze of a hand, or the warmth in an eye. Your nearest and dearest would seem like complete strangers.

The list continued. Faith forced herself to take it all in. *Depression. Agitation. Inappropriate social behaviour. Wandering off. Incontinence.* Every deprivation was another door closing, shutting the sufferer out from the brightness of life, from the warmth of human contact.

Of course, Marianne would have every care. Ruth would do everything she could to alleviate any suffering. And she – well, of course she would do the same. But how would that work, in practical terms, given all her commitments at St James's? *I'll cross that bridge when I come to it. Thy will be done.*

There was no cure for Alzheimer's; nothing that could provide more than a slight alleviation for the catalogue of symptoms. And it wasn't just Marianne who would suffer. The encroaching darkness, the loss of the personality – how could that not affect everyone around her?

Faith closed the laptop, shutting down the catalogue of misery. But she couldn't quite close down the train of thought that had just sprung up in her head: *What about me, when I'm Mum's age? Heredity is a factor. I, too, may well be affected. With no family, no children of my own, who will be there to care for me?*

"Hello?" A faint call reached Faith's ears. Someone was tapping on the front door. She pushed the laptop away and went to open it.

It was Pat who was standing on the step, one hand raised. She'd been using her knuckles, rather than the heavy brass knocker. An uncharacteristically low-profile approach.

"So sorry, dear," she said in a husky voice, her lips working and her little eyes swimming with moisture. "I was trying not to make too much racket. I really didn't want to wake you. I just knocked lightly, in case you were still asleep. I didn't know if you were up, you see."

It was most unusual – unknown, even – for Pat to waffle like this. Faith's first reaction on seeing her had been one of irritation. Her collusion with Jeremy and George was going to be hard to forgive. But Pat was looking very distressed. Faith had never seen her quite so discombobulated before. Perhaps there was something else – something more serious – on the churchwarden's mind.

"Well – I am up, though I wasn't expecting visitors quite so early," Faith said. "I've just finished breakfast. Would you like to come in and have some tea? Or coffee? Only instant, I'm afraid."

"No, dear, no. I don't want anything. It's just – I have to talk to you. I've been awake all night." Pat's face was rather blotchy. She looked as if she'd been weeping. "This is so difficult," she began, shifting from foot to foot.

Faith's heart sped up as an impossible thought arose. Was the churchwarden about to divulge some important information about Sal Hinkley? Faith pictured Ben, his steely blue eyes alight with triumph as he whispered: *Told you, Fay. No one's above suspicion.*

"Take your time, Pat. Come in and sit down." Faith moved aside to allow her into the hall.

"No, no. I can say what I have to say perfectly well from here."

"Whatever you prefer, Pat." Faith waited.

"The thing is…" Pat's voice caught and she had to clear her throat. "Yesterday, I was mortified to have upset you so much. Over the issue of the painting. We don't always see eye-to-eye – we're chalk and cheese, vicar, in so many ways – but I hope you understand that I acted according to my conscience. I only wanted what's best for the church."

Faith took a breath and felt her shoulders drop. "I know that, Pat. I'm sorry if I was rude yesterday."

"There's no need for *you* to apologize," said Pat. "What I did was wrong. Ve*rrry* wrong. I went against the democratic vote of our council. I did not consult you, our vicar, about the changes to the back cover of our booklet. I can see no option but to hand in my resignation as churchwarden."

"Pat!" Faith was so shocked that she had to lean against the door jamb. "Absolutely not."

Pat's cheeks quivered.

"But how – how can we continue to work together? When I… betrayed you like that?"

Faith hesitated a moment before replying. It was crucial to find the right words to reassure Pat that their relationship could be rebuilt. Best to be honest, not to try to gloss over how she had felt.

"I will be quite straight with you, Pat. I was very upset.

Very frustrated indeed with the way the issue has been handled. But what's done is done, and I think we mustn't dwell on it." She reached out and touched Pat's arm. "I know how much you care for the church. And always have done. It's *unthinkable* for you to resign as churchwarden."

"Oh!" Pat was fumbling for her hanky. "Oh, dear me. I don't know what to say!"

Well – that's a first! Faith refrained from smiling. The moment was a delicate one. She must take Pat's feelings very seriously. She pressed the churchwarden's arm and said, "I would only ask that we are open and honest with each other in future. It may be uncomfortable, sometimes, but it's always the best policy."

"I know, I know." Pat blew her nose. "I absolutely agree. I don't know what I was thinking of."

Faith patted her arm. "We all make mistakes."

Pat managed a watery smile. "We can't afford to fall out, not with the anniversary tomorrow. We've all got to pull together."

"Indeed we have!"

Over Pat's shoulder, Faith saw that a delivery van had pulled up at the vicarage gate. The driver was coming up the path, his hands full of paperwork. It was probably the new bell ropes. They were long overdue, and when she'd chased them up on the phone yesterday, reminding the manufacturers that they'd be needed for the celebrations on Sunday, they had promised to send them out first thing today.

"It's going to be all hands to the pump, as my father used to say," Faith continued. "But I hope you'll forgive me, Pat, if I choose a man and not you to help with hanging the new bell ropes? I think they may have just arrived."

It took a moment for Faith's attempt at humour to sink in, but as soon as Pat got the joke she gave a slightly hysterical giggle. "Good g*rrr*ief! I like to think I can turn my hand to anything – but hanging bell ropes really is a man's job. You will be careful, won't you, Faith?"

Faith assured Pat that she would get someone – a male – to help with the installation, and promised to take no risks up in the belfry. Pat departed, looked a little more cheerful, and Faith signed for the delivery of the ropes. It was now just after eight o'clock. She thanked the driver and his mate for arriving so promptly with their cargo, and asked if they wouldn't mind carrying it through into the vestry. The men agreed, and she went back inside the vicarage to call Alfie Tarrent, the builder. The call went straight to voicemail. Alfie's blunt, slightly brusque voice informed Faith that … *there's no one available to take your call right now but please leave a message. Or you can call back in working hours between nine to five Monday to Friday. Thank you for calling Tarrents.*

She was too late. Of course the builder wouldn't be working today – Saturday. And at this early hour, he was probably still in bed. Alfie was an affable chap, but he wasn't a member of the congregation of St James's. It was far too much to ask that he come rushing over on his day off to hang the bell ropes. In desperation, Faith called Fred. He told her he was delighted to hear that the ropes had finally arrived, and that he would probably be able to help install them. He'd helped his dad out on the same job, back when he was a nipper. He promised to be at the church for ten o'clock, and Faith told him she would meet him there.

At ten o'clock, as she walked through the churchyard, all had gone quiet at Shoesmith's Farm. The builders must be taking another of their coffee breaks. Faith hurried through the church door and headed for the vestry. The bell ropes had been laid on the floor in neat coils. They were accompanied by leather sleeves, to protect them from wear and tear on the mountings up in the belfry, and colourful green-and-yellow sallies. There was also a tub of rope lubricant with them. Fred, who was usually always early for any assignment, was nowhere to be seen, so Faith sat down for a moment. The smell of the new hemp rope – fresh and earthy – permeated the whole vestry. She could have ordered polyester rope – it would have been a little cheaper – but everyone on the committee had agreed that a natural material was more fitting for St James's.

She was glad of this, now. The smell reminded her of the ship's chandlers where she used to buy odds and ends for the small yacht that she and Ben took out together, a few times, on the Solent. It was one of the few pastimes in which she could claim to be indisputably his superior, and she had unashamedly enjoyed seeing him as, for once, a fish out of water. It hadn't taken long, though, for him to take to it. Out sailing – alone together on the water, focusing on the constant adjustments necessary to keep the boat moving in the right direction, feeling the wind and the salt kiss of the spray on their faces… those were some of their best times.

The pneumatic drill started up again, clattering away in the distance. By ten fifteen, there was still no sign of Fred. Faith felt mildly worried. Fred wasn't a great fan of text messages – his large fingers found it difficult to pick out the letters on his phone – so she dialled his number. It rang for a couple of minutes and then went to voicemail. *He's on his way,* she thought. *He's set off, and he's forgotten to bring his mobile with him.*

At ten forty-five, Faith could wait no longer and her

anxieties were building. She set off to walk to Fred's home, a white and timber-framed cottage, which was situated on a small back lane a couple of hundred yards from the Green. The door was firmly closed, and the curtains on the front windows were pulled half shut against the intense sunlight. Faith peered in and saw the flicker of a TV screen in the sitting room. Fred would never have gone out and left it playing. He must be still at home. Had he forgotten that he said he'd meet her? Never. Fred wouldn't agree to help – and then just let the promise slip his mind. Plus, he hadn't answered his phone.

With a rising sense of unease, Faith knocked on the front door. "Fred? Are you there?"

Nothing.

She moved to the window, and tapped on the glass. Still nothing.

"Fred?" Faith called again. She was becoming very tense, and her voice sounded a little higher than usual as it echoed in the warm, still air.

Faith followed the brick path around the side of the cottage, her feet brushing through the marigolds and love-in-a-mist that were spilling out of their narrow beds of earth. Perhaps he was in the back garden. He might have started pottering out there, tidying things up and doing a bit of weeding, and just forgotten the time.

There was no sign of Fred in the immaculate garden either. Faith was feeling a little breathless, her worries coalescing into something stronger as she remembered Fred's diagnosis with Type 2 diabetes. Could it be that his condition had suddenly worsened? A sudden drop in blood sugar, and he might have fainted. Banged his head even. The diagnosis was recent enough that he might not have recognized the danger signals.

At the back of the cottage, the blind at the kitchen window was pulled right up. Inside, a smashed blue-and-white mug lay on the floor in a puddle of coffee. "Oh, no!" Faith gasped, rushing to the back door. She turned the handle and, to her intense relief, found that the door wasn't locked.

"Fred? Where are you?" she shouted as she pushed inside.

He wasn't in the kitchen. But a strange croaking noise was coming from the hall. Her heart in her mouth, Faith crossed the kitchen and flung the door open to see the churchwarden lying on his side by the telephone table. His face was scarlet, and he appeared to be breathing with some difficulty.

Faith crouched beside him, fumbling in her pocket for her mobile. *He's having a heart attack.*

She pressed the nine button three times, and waited for what seemed like an eternity for the emergency line switchboard to pick up.

Fred made an odd moaning noise.

"Don't move," she said. "I'm calling for an ambulance."

"No – no!" Fred gasped. "I'm… all right."

"*What's your emergency?*" A woman's voice with a strong West Country accent spoke in Faith's ear.

"Ambulance, please!"

Fred spluttered, shaking his head. "Faith, it's my back."

"Hold on one second," Faith said to the emergency operator. "Your back?"

"*Hello?*" said the operator.

Faith touched Fred's shoulder. "No!" Fred groaned. "Don't touch me, vicar. I've done my back in."

"I'm sorry," she said to the emergency operator. "I thought I'd walked in on a major emergency, but I think we're OK. Relatively speaking."

"Are you sure?"

"Yes. I'll get back to you if there are any further issues." Faith cut the call and put her phone back in her pocket. "Your *back?*"

"I'm in agony," Fred whispered. "It's always like this when it first happens. It'll ease up in a bit. I'll have to stay down here, though, till it does. Sorry, Faith. I've let you down."

Faith sat on the bottom of the stairs to wait for the spasm to wear off. Fred was clearly in great pain, but at least his life wasn't in danger.

"How did it happen?" she said. "Were you lifting something heavy? You must be careful, Fred, if you've got a bad back."

Fred sighed. "I was making a cup of coffee before I came over to the church. I always have two sugars – I know I shouldn't, what with the diabetes and all, but I just can't break the habit – and the sugar bowl was empty. I was just bending down to get another bag out of the store cupboard – and it just went. Always the way. It hasn't happened for a couple of years."

"I should have come earlier," Faith said. "I'm so sorry. I had no idea."

"I think it's easing up a bit," Fred muttered. With great caution he rolled onto his knees. "Phew! That's a bit better."

"No bell ropes for you, then," Faith said, feeling slightly weak with relief. "What you need is complete rest."

Fred gave her a look of dismay. "What a time for this to happen!"

Faith assured him everything would be fine. After a few moments, he had recovered enough to shamble through to the living room, bent double and leaning heavily on her arm. She helped him to settle on the sofa.

"I'll make you another cup of coffee – with two sugars, if you insist – and then you can just relax and forget about everything," she said. "I'll find someone else to help out with the ropes, don't worry."

Fred closed his eyes and heaved a long sigh. "The manufacturers will have sent some instructions with them, I expect. And there's an old brown exercise book in the cupboard in the vestry. From back in my dad's day. There's some notes in there from the last time we changed the ropes. It's not as straightforward as you might think."

Faith was quite sure that even with the aid of the exercise book she would be completely incompetent at hanging the ropes – besides which, she was not good at all with heights. In fact, since she had taken on the cure of souls at St James's, she had never once dared to climb up to the belfry and peek down through the floorboards at the dizzying drop to the flagstones of the church below.

"I don't want you going up there. It's definitely not a job for a lady," Fred was saying. "You must give Gavin Wythenshaw a ring. He's your man. Very practical. Used to be a tree surgeon before they opened the B&B."

The sun was reaching full strength as Gavin Wythenshaw drove up to the church gate just before noon. He jumped out of the car and came to join Faith outside the porch. She thanked him profusely for coming over at short notice. As the sunlight lit up his face, her suspicions of the day before took on a distinctly torrid aftertaste. Gavin Wythenshaw might be protective, but surely he was not a killer. Indeed, despite Ben's treatment of Daniel, he seemed very relaxed and cheerful as he stepped back and squinted up at the bell tower.

"Should be no problem," he said. "I've brought my old safety harness, and a ladder – but there's a staircase up into the tower, if I remember rightly?"

"There is indeed. I don't think you'll need a ladder," Faith replied. "I can't thank you enough for this, Gavin. You must have so many other important things to do today. I know how busy it gets at the B&B at the weekend."

Gavin grinned and assured her it was a pleasure to be able to help out. "I should be thanking you for all the support you've given us over this police investigation. Bella was going out of her mind until you came over the other day."

He buckled himself into the safety harness while Faith went to get the instruction sheet and the old exercise book Fred had described. She gave them to Gavin and unlocked the small door at the bottom of the spiral staircase that led to the belfry.

"The steps are very uneven, I'm afraid. And please be careful when you get up into the loft – I believe that some of the floor is missing and they tell me it could be very easy to fall. That's why we keep the door locked."

Gavin looked at her. "You mean you haven't been up there?"

Faith suppressed a shiver at the thought of it. "I get terrible vertigo. I'm sorry that I've got to ask you to do it."

"Don't worry about me. You're talking to a man who's shinned up some of the tallest trees in the county, before I became a dad and Bella vetoed that kind of shenanigans! But Faith – you really should come up with me and take a look. It's your church, after all!" Gavin ducked through the doorway and held out his hand to her. "Come on, be brave."

Faith swallowed. She remembered how Ben had paused for a moment before he first stepped on board a yacht with her.

She'd teased him, using just about the same words that Gavin had used to her.

"Well. OK. Just for a quick look."

The stone staircase was too small for them to climb side by side, so Faith followed Gavin's quick footsteps. Despite his confidence, Faith found it a very claustrophobic and unnerving climb. There was no handrail, and the stone risers were uneven in height and width. She imagined one misplaced footfall and she would trip, crashing into the rough stones of the wall as she tumbled round and round the staircase and back down to the church floor. As they climbed higher the spiral grew narrower, and the walls seemed to press closer. Sweat bloomed on Faith's face.

When they reached the top, her legs were shaking so much she couldn't climb out from the staircase and onto the wooden floor of the belfry. She stood on the last-but-one step, crouching down and holding tight onto the floorboards with both hands. She felt so *stupid.* A few feet away the great bronze bells hung ponderously from their iron mounting. It was very hot up here, so hot that she could hardly breathe. Thick wooden slats in the sides of the tower let in bars of sunlight, making bold, striped patterns across the floor. Outside, she could hear that birds were flitting about and chirping in the tops of the yew trees. One small glimpse between the boards at the vestry flagstones below and she had to look away, fighting off a gut-churning nausea.

Gavin seemed oblivious to her fear. "This all looks great," he said, leaning out over the void in the centre of the belfry and tugging at the existing bell ropes. "I'll just get these off, and then I'll come back down and bring the new ones up."

"Please be careful," Faith said, trying not to look at him.

One wrong move, and he would drop like a stone and hit the vestry floor beneath them.

Faith's mouth was dry and the sweat on her limbs had turned icy cold. She forced herself to climb up the last two steps and stand upright.

"No worries," Gavin was saying, swinging himself back to safety. "I've got the harness. I'll clip myself on to that railing there, when I start work."

He turned around suddenly and took a step towards her.

"Have you got plans for these old ropes?" he asked, with a smile.

Faith tried to calm her ragged breathing. "'Cos I'd love to take them back for Bella. She was asking me if I had any spare rope the other day. She's redecorating some of our bedrooms, and she wants vintage ropes as part of the scheme."

Faith forced a weak smile. "No plans," she muttered. "No plans at all. Help yourself."

Gavin was saying something about bats now. "See them, Faith? There's about six, up there in the corner. Fast asleep, all of them. Cute, eh?"

She struggled to focus on where he was pointing. There were indeed some dark little blobs hanging right up under the roof of the belfry.

"Are you all right? You've gone a bit green," Gavin said. "Not scared of bats, too, are you?"

Once, when Faith was about six years old, a bat had flown in through the kitchen door and fluttered around. Ruth had screamed with horror, beating it away with her hands and shouting that it would get stuck in her hair. And she, Faith, had watched in fascination as the tiny creature zigzagged around, deftly avoided the light fitting and all the kitchen paraphernalia on the shelves until it found the open window and escaped. She had even been able to hear the tiny squeaks of its echolocation then. Not any more. The flight of bats was silent for her now.

Her breathing was calmer; she was feeling much better. Gavin was looking at her with genuine concern on his face. "Not at all. I like bats and I'm very glad they're up here. Bats in the belfry. What could be more fitting? But how did they get in?"

Netting had been stretched over all the slats in the sides of the belfry to keep pigeons out.

Gavin laughed. "Ah, they're cheeky little beggars, bats. They can sneak in through the tiniest cracks. That mesh will keep the birds out, but the bats will find a way in. And you won't be able to get them out without a lot of trouble. They're a protected species, did you know? Well – I'd better get on. You're sure it's OK for us to have these ropes?"

"Please, help yourself." Faith eased herself back though the opening at the top of the staircase. "I'm sure we'll have no use for them."

The descent was easiest to make backwards. That way, Faith only had to look at the stone steps above her, and she could hang on to them too, and thus avoid any unsteadiness. Above her head, Gavin's boots echoed on the wooden floor.

Thank you, Lord, for restoring me to the surface of your good earth! she whispered, as her feet finally touched the smooth flagstones again. *And thank you, too, for restoring my confidence in Gavin.* She'd gotten carried away in the heat of an investigation. As she hurried to the vestry to attack the next flurry of Post-it notes on the clipboard, Faith found herself wondering what kind of decoration Bella could possibly create with a pile of old rope.

By three o'clock all but one of the new ropes were in place. The brightly striped green-and-yellow sallies looked most impressive as they dangled ready for the bell-ringers to tug as they created the first peal of the anniversary Sunday tomorrow. Gavin descended for a hurried a cup of tea, and then climbed back up to fix the last rope. Faith had achieved a great deal today. She gave herself to the deeply satisfying task of removing not just several Post-it notes, but even a couple of whole pages from the clipboard, crumpling them up and aiming them at the wastepaper basket in the vestry. *And the afternoon is still young…*

She got up and walked to the door to look out at the churchyard. The yew trees seemed almost to shimmer in the intense heat, and the air was full of their ancient, piny perfume. Faith took a deep breath. All was in harmony, and all would be well. *With God's help, I might just be able to bring it all together for tomorrow,* she thought, *if the rest of today goes smoothly.*

Her moment of equanimity was shattered by a screech of brakes at the church gate. A garish red car had just pulled up – Jeremy Taylor's brand new Jaguar. Jeremy leapt out and the door slammed. He crashed through the lychgate and headed up the path towards Faith.

"You've got a nerve!" he said with venom. Faith felt a drop of his spittle hit her cheek.

CHAPTER

12

"Whatever do you mean?" Faith pulled back her shoulders and strove to speak with a calm, level tone.

Something about having the huge edifice of the church at her back filled Faith with strength. Perhaps it was her experience in the force, dealing with sometimes very unfriendly people, or perhaps it was something in her nature, but she didn't feel in the slightest bit intimidated by the flushed and furious face of the PCC treasurer.

Jeremy's eyes narrowed. "How dare you put the *police* onto me? In what possible universe might you consider that to be appropriate?"

"Look, Jeremy," said Faith. "Why don't you come inside and we can talk this through properly? I don't really feel that the church porch is quite the right place to…"

"To what?" Jeremy spat. "To have a *scene*? Is that what you're implying? Your police inspector friend doesn't quite match up to your delicate sensibilities – let me tell you! *He* had no qualms about practically bashing my front door down and yelling at me to get out of bed this morning. *At six a.m.!*"

Faith's diaphragm leapt with unexpected laughter, but somehow she managed to contain it. *Oh, Ben! For once I can't criticize you for being overeager…*

"Jeremy, I really know nothing about this," she said, suppressing the urge to smile.

Jeremy's face twisted. "Let me jog your memory, Faith. You've been talking to Shorter, haven't you? About *private* church matters. You've discussed our *confidential* vote about the anniversary painting with him."

It all became clear. Ben was nothing if not thorough. After their conversation yesterday, and Faith's off-hand remark that he should check the PCC meeting minutes, he must have done just that. And he would have seen that Jeremy was the most ardent advocate for the use of Gwen Summerly's painting on the booklet cover. He would have seen that Jeremy had made several impassioned speeches to that effect before the vote was cast. And, true to form, Ben had wasted no time acting on his suspicions.

"Ah," said Faith.

"*Ah*, indeed! So don't come all holier-than-thou with me!" Jeremy hissed. His thin red face was glazed with sweat.

In spite of herself, Faith moved back towards the door. She had always sensed something a little unpleasant in Jeremy – in spite of his usual punctilious politeness – and now that unpleasantness had come boiling up to the surface and was confronting her face to face. But someone was coming up the path behind Jeremy. A tall old man with a shock of white hair.

"Hey! That'll do!" Percy Cartwright's normally quiet and restrained voice rang out under the yew trees. "That's no way to speak to a woman, Mr Taylor. Let alone our vicar!"

Jeremy glanced round and seemed to shrink a little in Faith's eyes. Percy was much taller than him – the older man's shoulders were broader, too, and his limbs had more substance. *The difference*, Faith thought, *between a man who has worked all his life at manual tasks and a man who has always sat at a desk.*

Percy was pushing a sack barrow, on which rested a very large cardboard box, which looked pretty heavy. Andrea was following a few paces behind him with a vast bunch of freshly picked summer flowers – roses and lilies and larkspurs. She looked alarmed.

"Hello there, Faith!" she called. "Is everything OK?"

Jeremy muttered something about *no, of course it wasn't OK and why should he be treated in this appalling manner, after all the good he was doing for the village – and above all for St James's?* He turned to Andrea with a sickly smile.

"Just a slight misunderstanding. I merely wished to make very plain that I have been misrepresented in a certain matter and that I have nothing whatsoever to hide," he said, and walked away, stepping off the path to avoid brushing against the flowers she was carrying.

"Oh dear!" Andrea's face was full of concern as she approached the porch. "What was all that about, Faith?"

"Nothing, just crossed wires," Faith reassured her. "What beautiful flowers!"

"Yes. For Percy's son – for his grave. We wanted to do something special for him before we leave. And – we have something for the church, too. A gift."

Percy Cartwright set down his cardboard box on the path and began to undo it. Faith gasped in delight as he revealed the lithe form of a prancing pony, sculpted in green-tinged bronze metal.

"We thought you might like to have it here," Andrea said. "Some of Percy's work is going into storage, but this one – well, it's a favourite of ours. We'd like it to be seen and enjoyed."

"It's absolutely beautiful," Faith said. "So lifelike!"

The pony was extraordinarily well portrayed. It was full of vibrant energy – so much so that it might just have pricked its delicate ears to catch the roar of Jeremy's car driving off around the Green. Every detail of its muscles and its long, graceful limbs was perfect. It would bring something very special to one of the quiet corners in Fred's new arbour in the commemorative garden. Children and adults alike would be drawn to it.

Faith said as much, and was surprised to see the old blacksmith blushing. Percy had always seemed so withdrawn – so lacking in any kind of drive or passion. And yet he had made this beautiful animal, which was the very essence of fire and dynamism.

"I'm so glad you like him!" Andrea said, with a warm smile. "It's taken from my old pony, you know. Eligius. He's living at the riding stables now. I can't ride much these days, and of course I can't take him to Lourdes with me."

"Eligius?" Faith's thoughts turned back to her encounter with the spirited grey pony the other day. "But I've met him! Young Emily Johnston's riding him now, isn't she? She looks so proud up there on his back."

"I know, I'm so pleased—" Andrea began, but Percy cut her off, saying that he was going back to the car.

"Will you take the flowers, my dear?" he said, his voice low and restrained again. "Please?"

"Of course, love. You go and wait for me. If you're sure you'll be all right?" Andrea grasped her husband's hand, but he pulled away from her and left the churchyard without a backward look.

"It's hard for him," Andrea said, "leaving Rory's resting place behind. But he's being incredibly brave. Faith – may I ask a huge favour of you?"

"Of course!" Faith said. *How sad*, she thought, *that I seem to be getting close to this lovely couple just as they're leaving...*

"I know it's a lot to ask, but would you mind awfully just looking over the grave now and then, and pulling up any weeds? It would mean so much to us – to Percy especially."

"Gladly," Faith said, at once. "It would be my pleasure. And whenever I do so I shall say a prayer for the three of you."

Andrea muttered that that would be lovely with a slight choke in her voice.

"Will you be coming tomorrow?" Faith asked, trying to lighten the tone a little. "We'd love to see you both at the anniversary celebrations."

"Alas, no," Andrea replied. "We've got so much to sort out. It's an absolute logistical nightmare, uprooting ourselves like this – and organization is the only thing that'll keep it all going smoothly."

Faith smiled and, thinking of all that must be done before the sun went down, said she was feeling a lot of empathy with Andrea around the issue of organization.

"Bless you!" Andrea said. "And now I really must go and – say goodbye to Rory."

As she watched Andrea head off towards the edge of the churchyard, Faith heard the echo of footsteps on the spiral staircase. Gavin Wythenshaw had finally finished his work. He came to join Faith in the porch, a coil of dusty old rope looped over his shoulder.

"That's Cartwright's missus, isn't it? Come to visit the grave?" He gazed over at Andrea's dark head, stooped over one of the gravestones. "Now that was a tragedy. Poor Rory. Head boy in the year above me at school, he was."

"I didn't know. What exactly happened to him?" Faith asked. Andrea was kneeling down on the dry grass now, her head bowed as if she were praying.

"He died in a car crash," Gavin said. "Awful. Just after he left school. Broke his dad's heart. I don't think old Percy's ever got over it."

"How could you?" Faith said. "If you had lost a child? I should think that must be the worst bereavement that anyone could suffer."

"Exactly. Doesn't bear thinking about." Gavin gave a little shiver, then reached to run a finger over the pony's bronze mane. "That's nice."

"It's one of Percy's. He's given it to the church."

"Well, there you go!" A smile flashed across Gavin's face. "He's got a fair old talent, our Percy. And we carry on, don't we? Whatever bad things happen in life, we have to carry on."

Faith nodded. "We do indeed. And I'm sure that they've made the right decision, to go Lourdes and start over again. Maybe the new location will give Percy a fresh lease of life."

Gavin nodded. "Absolutely. Well – I'd better be on my way."

Faith thanked him once again for his help. "I don't know what I would have done without you today, Gavin. The bell-ringers will be thrilled when they come in tomorrow and see what you've done."

"No problem." Gavin grinned. "Always a pleasure to help you out."

"Just one thing," Faith continued. "What *does* Ruth intend to do with those ropes? I'm intrigued."

"Oh, one of her creative projects, you know," Gavin said, with a slightly comical raise of his eyebrows. "We've got four-posters in a couple of our rooms. She's had a bit of olde-worlde drapery up there – ropes and tassels and stuff. Anyway, she thought they needed a lift."

"I see," Faith said. "I sometimes wish I could be more creative. It's not really a strong point of mine."

Gavin was quiet for a moment, his brow creased in thought, and then he said, "Thanks, anyway. By the way – how's the arbour going, in the new garden? Did Fred manage to finish it before he conked out?"

"Gosh – no. I should have added it to my list of things to be done. There's still a few trees to go in, I think. Fred's been struggling to break up the sun-baked soil for a few days now. It was probably all that digging that weakened his back – and then bending to reach in the cupboard finished him off."

"Tell you what. I'll pop back with Daniel later, after tea. We'll get those last trees in the ground for you. He'll enjoy that."

"I couldn't ask you to do that – you've given so much of your time already!" Faith said, mentally kicking herself for the oversight. *This is too much! Gavin's being too generous. If I'd been a bit more* organized *I would have rung around some of the other parishioners this morning, and found someone else.*

"Not a bit of it!" Gavin said, with a wink. He set off down the path. "See you later."

Faith watched him walk to his car. She waited a little longer, until Andrea had also left the churchyard, before going back inside to carry on with her preparation for tomorrow.

She would need to crack on if she was going to make it to Ben's in time for dinner.

CHAPTER

13

Ben's apartment was situated in a newly built complex of low-rise flats close to the river, on the south side of Winchester. It wasn't a part of the city that Faith was familiar with, and as she walked up to the communal entrance of his block on Saturday evening she thought that the buildings, with their bland grey walls and gleaming windows, looked rather impersonal. They might soften with age – and the young shrubs and trees that were planted all round would help, too, when they had grown a bit bigger. But Ben probably liked the location just as it was. *No frills, nothing surplus to requirements.*

Standing on the step, Faith felt a sudden anxious churning in her gut. Why had she thought this was a good idea? She turned away from the panel of entry buzzers to smooth down her hair.

What are you doing? Stop it, Faith!

Bad enough that she thought fit to get dressed up for something that absolutely was not an occasion which required her to make an effort – but don't keep fussing! It was nothing more than a misplaced vanity.

Saturday afternoon had finished on a high, with all tasks completed. Everything was in place now for the anniversary celebrations tomorrow. As long as everyone involved turned up on time, and performed their roles as agreed, the day should be a success. Faith had torn the last sheet from the clipboard, crumpled it, chucked it at the bin – and gone back to the vicarage to change for her supper with Ben.

Getting ready should have been a relatively simple process. A plain cotton skirt and cream blouse were lying on the bed ready for her to put on. But once Faith had stepped out of the shower, rubbed her wet hair with a towel and gone through to the bedroom, she found herself suddenly wanting to look for a less conservative option. There wasn't much choice in her wardrobe these days. Simple, easy-care outfits that wouldn't draw attention to her appearance were a priority. She riffled through the hangers and found, right at the back, a yellow summer dress patterned with white birds, and a narrow white belt. It reminded her of more carefree times spent by the sea. A pair of strappy sandals completed the look.

Now, standing on Ben's doorstep, she felt a little foolish. He was just a friend – an old acquaintance – and she'd dressed herself up as if she was heading for a romantic stroll along a windswept beach path. So inappropriate – so wrong, just like her decision to agree to dinner at all.

It wasn't too late to jump in the Yaris and go home. But that would be very mean-spirited, when Ben had probably gone to some trouble to cook for her. Faith steeled herself to press the buzzer and speak her name into the entryphone. The door to the lobby clicked open, letting her into the building.

Ben's flat was on the top floor. He was waiting for her in the front doorway.

"Good to see you," he said, his eyes flicking over the dress's length and, for a second, she fancied, the slightly low-cut décolletage. He touched her elbow, guiding her swiftly though into the hall with all the adroitness of a ballroom dancer.

He was wearing the familiar aftershave – she'd noticed it before, on the morning Sal's body had been found. But here, indoors, the citrus scent was much more intense. It was disorientating; like being suddenly transported back in time. Or perhaps – in some strange way, *forward* in time. To a possible future where that smell of his aftershave might become a regular part of her life again. Faith pushed the thought away.

"Only ten minutes late, Fay. That'll be a record, surely," Ben said, a wry smile on his lips. "Can I get you a drink?"

The dizzy feeling steadied a little. "No thanks, Ben. I'll wait till we eat, if that's OK."

"No problem. All set for tomorrow?" he asked.

"Absolutely. A minor miracle, but with the help of my wonderful parishioners, I think I've managed to pull it all together." Faith refrained from mentioning that it was Gavin who had been the most helpful of all.

"Of course you have," Ben said. "You're one of the most capable women I know."

Impossible not to feel a little stab of pain at the "*one of*". What about Harriet, the red-haired pathologist? Presumably she came pretty high on the list of capable women Ben had "known".

"Is there something I can help you with?" Faith said, quickly, trying to banish Harriet's tall, elegant figure from her mind. He wouldn't have invited her over if there was still something going on, surely? "A salad, or something?"

"Absolutely not. You've been hard at it all day. I came off shift at two o'clock, and I've had nothing to do but lounge around the kitchen with my chopping knife. Why don't you have a look around while I open the wine? I'd like to know what you think of the place."

Ben went into the kitchen. Faith turned in the opposite direction and found herself in a spacious living area. It was very modern – minimal, almost – with a large window onto the yellowish, hot evening sky. Under the window a table was already laid for two, with white china, gleaming cutlery, and crisp white napkins. In the middle of the table stood a glass bud vase with a single, long-stemmed white rose. Ben, making sure that every little detail was perfect. Even though this wasn't, not in any shape or form, a *date*.

From the kitchen, Faith heard the *pop* of a cork. *Sparkling wine, then. Maybe even champagne.* She took a few steps around the room. The sofa was new. It was very plain, and covered in a maroon woollen fabric that both looked, and felt, expensive. Ben wasn't shy of splashing out on something of good quality, if he really liked it. The striped woollen cushions, though – Faith caught her breath as she noticed them – weren't new. They'd bought them from a department store when they moved in together to the little rented flat they'd shared. And he'd kept them. Did he acknowledge their history, she wondered, or were they simply cushions to him?

"Fay? Can you put some music on?" Ben called from the kitchen.

"Sure," she answered. She went over to the music centre on the bookshelf. It was a combined MP3 and CD player – not the old cassette-and-CD machine that that she remembered.

"What would you like to hear?" she called back.

"Whatever you like," came back the reply. "You choose."

Faith looked along the row of CDs on the shelving unit. The smooth wood of the shelf was a little dusty. Ben, for all his strong sense of order and neatness, was not very interested in going around with the duster. But there was one smallish rectangle where there was no dust. *A picture-frame,* she guessed. *One he's recently moved. A photo of Harriet, maybe?*

In the middle of the CD line-up, Faith saw an Emmylou Harris album. She pulled it out and slotted the disc into the machine. The singer's sweet voice drifted out into the warm air. Perfect, for a summer evening. Faith and Ben used to listen to her in the car, when they were driving back to the rented flat after work. A perfect antidote to the stress and clamour of a long day with the force.

"Ni-ice!" Ben said, coming into the room with a champagne flute in each hand.

"Is dinner ready?" Faith asked, rather sharply, as Ben handed her one of the glasses. He was clearly ignoring her request to wait until the food was ready. And then she wished she hadn't been quite so abrupt. She could always just take one polite sip and then hold back. Why did he always have this uncanny ability to bring out the worst in her?

"Almost. I know you said you didn't want anything before we ate, but *I* need a drink. And it's a shame if you miss the best of the bubbles. Oh, and don't panic. It's only Prosecco, not champers." Ben winked and returned to the kitchen.

Faith took a tiny sip. It was extremely good – but she must be careful. The bubbles of the sparkling wine would transport alcohol straight into her bloodstream, intoxicating her far more quickly than an ordinary glass of vino. She walked around the room, absently looking for any further evidence of a woman's presence, but there was nothing. Just that telltale patch of dust-free shelf. She put her glass down on the table and made her way to the hall.

"Bathroom, Ben?"

"Sorry. Should have shown you. Second on the left," he called. "Clean towel for you under the sink."

Faith used the loo and washed her hands. No second toothbrush in the glass, no make-up remover or spare lipstick or perfume. Just a man's razor, some aftershave – *that same, oh-so-familiar, unsettling scent* – a male deodorant and a packet of generic painkillers. As she returned to the hall she gave a quick glance through the open door of the bedroom. Two pairs of Ben's shoes, lined up next to the wall. A man's summer dressing gown, striped with pale and dark blue, flung down on the smooth white bedcover. So no evidence of a woman's presence there, either. Why it was so important to convince herself, she didn't know.

She went back into the hall and scrutinized the two poster-sized pieces of artwork that hung there. One was an architectural drawing of a suspension bridge, and the other a detailed cut-through diagram of a large sailing yacht.

Very Ben, of course. Practical, and down to earth.

"Admiring my pictures?" Ben emerged from the kitchen carrying his glass of Prosecco and a flat basket containing Asian spring rolls. "That's the kind of art I like. Can't be doing with all that wishy-washy stuff."

He grinned at her, and carried the food through into the living space. Faith followed him and sat down at the table. She picked up her glass and took another sip.

"That's not quite how I remember you, Ben," she said. "Didn't we visit galleries together, back in the day? I seem to remember you had quite an eye for colour, and brushwork?"

"Ah, well." Ben picked up his glass, too, and chinked it against hers. "That was then, Fay. That was back in the long-ago and far-away time when I was still trying to impress you. Grab yourself one of these spring rolls. It's my latest recipe. I think you'll like it."

The delicious spring rolls – Ben must have spent most of the afternoon chopping and shaving the crisp, delicate curls of different vegetables that filled them – were followed by a whole sea bass, perfectly spiced and steamed in a whole banana leaf. It was a long time since Faith had enjoyed such healthy, delicious food.

"Where on earth did you manage to find a banana leaf in Winchester?" Faith asked him, as she chased the last morsel of the fragrant, tender fish across her plate. "Surely climate change hasn't gone quite that far yet?"

Ben laughed. "I have my sources," he said.

He leaned forward to pour Faith a third glass of wine, but she slipped her hand over the glass.

"I mustn't. I've got to drive back."

"We could call you a cab."

"No, really, Ben. I need a clear head for tomorrow."

Ben put the bottle down. "I dare say you do. I suppose the noxious Mr Taylor will be hanging around, as usual? At your celebrations?"

Clearly Jeremy had not made a good impression in his interview. "What did you make of him?"

"Not a lot." Ben's face darkened a little. "He's the kind of man I particularly dislike. A two-faced hypocrite. I could tell he was furious with me for waking him up when I went to the farm first thing this morning – and yet he went out of his way to ingratiate himself. Faffed around making me coffee and trying to pretend he was delighted to see me. *Oh, officer – please do excuse the mess. With all this building work, it's impossible to keep the dust levels down…*"

"You're right. He was furious. He came to the church this afternoon and tried to offload onto me." Faith remembered the barely suppressed fury in Jeremy's face, and the snide little smile that replaced it when he saw that the Cartwrights were observing him.

"I'm not at all surprised. I've met his sort before. A true bully, when he thinks he can get away with it. What do they think of him in the village?"

"He's had a mixed reception," Faith said, thinking back over many conversations she had overheard among her parishioners. "Many people were delighted when he bought Shoesmith's Farm. There's such a sad history there, and the old place had become so run down – derelict, almost, while Trevor was still alive. It really needs a lift – a complete makeover, if you like. But then – there are some diehards in the village who are opposed to anything new. When he put his planning application in there were an awful lot of objections."

"Ha! He bent my ear about that for at least half an hour," Ben said. "Delaying tactics to put off the interview, of course. Apparently he wants to replace one whole wall of the barn with a sliding glass panel – sounds all right to me, but doesn't exactly scream 'farmyard', does it?"

"Do you think he could be involved in some way in Sal's death? It took place on his property, after all. And you say that he was trying to put off the questioning."

Ben sighed. "I wouldn't trust a man like Jeremy Taylor as

far as I could throw him. But he has a watertight alibi for the night Sal was murdered. He was with your lady churchwarden – Pat Montesque – until after ten o'clock. She's confirmed it. So he's in the clear."

"What?" Faith dropped her knife and fork. "Pat and Jeremy? Spending a whole evening together? You're kidding."

"Absolutely not."

"You don't think… there's something going on between them?" Faith asked. It was hard to believe, but Pat had been acting a little strangely. And might it also explain how flustered and emotional Pat was, when she'd come to apologize that morning?

Ben shrugged. "Who knows? Maybe it's just a – friendship thing. Such things do go on. Strange as it may seem."

He looked down at the tablecloth. The Emmylou Harris CD had come to an end and the room was very quiet. Something unspoken hung in the air between them. *Is this a friendship, what we are sharing now, this evening, or is it something more?*

"You know what," Faith said, "I think I might have another glass of wine after all. Why not?"

Ben reached for the wine bottle to pour for her and at the very same moment a mobile phone started vibrating on the bookshelf. Ben's phone – Faith's was safely in her handbag. *A work call, of course!* Faith couldn't help smiling to herself. *This really is like old times!* Ben put down the bottle and got up to answer it. He picked up the handset and looked down at the screen, frowning.

"Is it work?" Faith asked. "Has something come up?"

"It's Hattie," Ben said. He pressed a button on the phone and put it back on the shelf. "No sweat."

Hattie. A pet name for Harriet – of course.

"Shouldn't you take it?" Faith asked. "It could be work. Couldn't it?"

A burning flush of shame stung her cheeks as soon as she'd said it. *Too late, too bloomin' late, Faith Morgan, to bite back those words. Of course it's not work.*

Ben shook his head. "It's OK."

He stared down at the tablecloth, a deep furrow between his eyebrows.

"Look, I – maybe I should go," Faith said, willing the tide of blood to retreat from her cheeks. "It's a big day tomorrow."

"Really?" Ben got up from the table. "I was just about to make coffee. But if you need to get away…" His tone an absolute echo of hers. Light, empty, emotionless.

"Yes. I do. Thank you so much for tonight. I really appreciate it." Faith got up too, fumbling for her handbag. She was suddenly swamped with a wave of searing emotion – something that felt almost like grief. Grief for the lost moments of empathy between them, just now. At all costs Ben must not see how close to the edge she was.

"Lovely food," she said, keeping her face a little turned away as he followed her into the hall. "And I like the flat. I really do. It's very you. No need to come down, Ben. I'll see myself out."

CHAPTER

14

Faith was hurrying through a dark wood, following a narrow path. Tall trees grew thickly all around her, blocking out the sunlight, but it was very hot under the thick canopy of leaves. Her footfalls sank into the leaf mould that lay on the ground beneath her. Branches brushed against her arms, and every now and then her foot caught on a thick, gnarled tree root. She was trying to get to the cathedral of St James of Compostela. Somewhere, just beyond all these trees, she would find the towering, glorious façade. She was sure of that. If she could just keep going, she would find it.

The leaves beside her rustled, and she caught a glimpse of a man's bearded face peering at her between the branches. His voice, deep and sonorous, rang in her ears. *You have missed something, Faith. You must go back. Go back right away!*

Who are you? What have I missed? Faith tried to ask, but her voice was trapped in her throat.

He was a dark-haired man with yellowy-brown eyes, clad in a long robe, and he was watching her with an expression of sorrow on his sunburnt face. *There is something you have overlooked, Faith,* he said, his eyes on hers, and her chest tightened with a great swell of emotion.

It's Ben he means! I forgot to bring Ben with me. He needs to see the cathedral of St James. Once he stands in the shadow of those great carved towers that reach right up to heaven he will understand. Everything will become clear to him – and we can be together again, as we should be…

The bearded man was walking away from her now, heading back along the path in the direction she had just come from. *Faith!* he called to her, looking over his shoulder. *Turn back, that you may discover what it is you have overlooked. Now! Now! NOW!*

His deep voice was morphing into a strange, high-pitched yowl. A terrible sense of fear – of some impending doom that she could not fully understand, didn't want to understand – was weighing on Faith's chest. *I can't breathe. How can I get to the cathedral if I can't breathe?*

She gasped, flailing her arms desperately against the clinging leaves that surrounded her – and suddenly found herself bathed in an intense light. It was morning, the sun was shining directly onto her face, and she had woken up in her bed at the vicarage. The wood, the bearded man, the cathedral, were all just a dream.

"*What?*" she croaked, gazing into the almond-shaped yellow eyes of the Beast, who was crouching on her chest and staring intently at her. "What are you doing up here?"

"*Meoow!*" the cat replied, kneading her throat with his front paws.

"Get down, you naughty fellow."

Faith pushed the sheet aside and heaved herself into a sitting position. The Beast obligingly jumped down from her and trotted towards the door, his tail an arrogant question mark. It was six-thirty in the morning, according to her alarm clock. Sun was streaming in through the curtains, the birds were singing outside in the garden – but the strange, intense emotion of the dream still filled her body. And the bearded man's voice was still ringing inside her head. *There is something you have overlooked…*

She got up and went to sit on the stool in front of the dressing table. Her hair was rumpled as if she had been tossing and turning all night, and her face looked very pale. She showered quickly, then smoothed on some moisturizer and wondered if it was a good idea to add just a touch of mascara and lipstick, given that it was the anniversary celebrations today.

She thought back over last night. Ben had made no attempt to try to keep her there. It was almost as if – once Harriet's phone call had come through – he'd lost all interest in Faith.

Dreams were strange things. Manifestations of the subconscious, that's all. Odd, though – and strangely appropriate, given that it was the day of the anniversary – that she had been dreaming of the cathedral of St James. And maybe she had invented the bearded man as a manifestation of St James…

"Meeeow!" The Beast was back, slinking around the bedroom door and winding his soft, furry body around her legs, as if to say: *I'll tell you what you've overlooked. My breakfast!*

"All right, your majesty!" Faith said, scratching his head.

She went over to the wardrobe to put on her formal clerical ensemble, ready for the Sunday morning Eucharist service that would be the first event of this very special day. Activity was the best way, surely, to dispel the sense of unease that still plagued her. The sense that there was something missing, and that if only she thought hard enough, she would be able to recall what it was. *Please Lord, let it not be something for the anniversary celebrations that I've forgotten!*

A few thin clouds were drifting across the sky as Faith emerged from the front door, her coffee mug still in her hand. She was intending to finish her coffee as she strolled over to the church. *The last thing we need today is rain – it would be such a shame, after all the days of perfect sunshine we've been having...*

Farrah Jordan and her husband, Jasper, were unloading the Free Foods van at the vicarage gate. As planned, they were about to set up their mini-marquee in Faith's garden.

"Morning, Faith!" said Farrah. "Would you like a croissant with your coffee?"

"That would be lovely," Faith said, as her stomach gave an alarming rumble.

Once again this morning her fridge at the vicarage had been almost empty – containing nothing but milk, ice cubes and a couple of eggs she hadn't had time to cook.

Farrah folded a croissant into a paper napkin. "It's a beautiful day," she said.

Faith bit into the croissant, leaning forward just a little so the crumbs would fall clear of her clerical gown. "What do you think about those clouds? Are they going to stay with us?"

Jasper shook his head. "I doubt it. They'll soon burn off. Thanks for being our first happy customer of the day," he said. "Hope it goes well for you, Faith." He heaved an armful of poles onto his shoulder and headed off over the lawn to start building the marquee.

"I hope so too," Faith said to Farrah. "I have this awful feeling of impending disaster. I'm sure I've forgotten to do something absolutely vital."

Farrah laughed, her white teeth flashing. "I know that feeling so well," she said. "I have it just about every day, when I'm baking. Have I added all the ingredients? Did I phone through that order for extra flour? Did I remember to set the timer on the oven? Lists, Faith, that's the key!"

Faith explained that she had been living off lists for the last week. "Unfortunately I tore up the last of them yesterday afternoon, when I'd completed the final task."

"So what do you have to worry about, then?" Farrah said, as she watched Faith cram more croissant as elegantly as possible into her mouth.

Faith headed off for the churchyard. As she walked under one of the ancient yew trees, the churchyard robin flew down and hopped beside her for a few steps, going after the crumbs from her croissant.

He fixed her with his bright dark eye for a second – a wise and almost human gaze, as if he had understood exactly what she was feeling – and Faith felt a sudden return of optimism. *Farrah's right. I've done everything.*

The tiny bird flitted away, and Faith walked up to the porch. The door was open, and Pat was inside, laying booklets out on a trestle table. She looked up anxiously.

"The bell-ringers are here," she said. "They're f*rrr*ightfully early. They wanted to come and check out the new ropes."

Pat's gaze fell to the table again and she picked up a handful of booklets and started rearranging them nervously. She was clearly still not quite at ease after their confrontation the other day. A buzz of voices echoed from the tower, but Faith paused for a moment before she went over there. There was still some ground to be made up between her and Pat.

"Pat – I'm so glad it's you holding the fort here in the porch. A good welcome for everyone is so important on a day like today."

"Well – I shall do my best, of course," Pat mumbled, and her cheeks turned a little pink. She looked rather pleased, if somewhat embarrassed.

The bell-ringers were gathered at the bottom of the tower, admiring the bright, woollen sallies that hung down on the ends of the new ropes.

"These are just the ticket," Joe Farley, the oldest bell-ringer, told Faith. "I never thought I'd see the day we'd have such finery here in St James's."

"Not too bright for you, Joe?" Faith asked.

"Not a bit of it! We shall ring our finest changes ever for the anniversary, shan't we, Tom?" Joe replied.

Tom, Joe's grandson and the youngest of the bell-ringers at fifteen – he was a very promising new recruit, much to the delight of the old guard, who between them shared almost two centuries of experience at St James's – nodded eagerly and gazed up into the belfry as if he couldn't wait to hear how the old bells would sound with their new ropes attached.

"Not long now," Faith told him. "I have just one more thing to put in place and you can start the peal to alert everyone it's time for the morning service."

Faith went over to the vestry. Sal's painting was there, leaning against the wall. Faith unfurled the bubble wrap that encased it and carried it out into the main chancel. There was a niche just under one of the stained-glass windows – the newly restored Lamb of God window – where it would look perfect.

If it couldn't be a part of the booklet, at least its sombre, glowering beauty would be visible throughout the celebrations.

The bells had scarcely begun to ring out their glorious clamour of high, clear notes across Little Worthy before the church began to fill up. The atmosphere was electric as the families began to file in through the porch, everyone, young and old, clasping a commemorative booklet.

Two little boys – Faith recognized Peter Gray's young sons, Dan and Charlie – pushed past the crowd in the porch and ran up and down the aisles, shouting with excitement. The Wythenshaws had come in a few moments before, and Daniel hurried up to the two lads, a finger on his lips.

"Shhh!" Faith heard him say. "This is the church. We have to be quiet."

The boys giggled with delight and copied Daniel's action, shouting: "Shhhh! Shhhh!" and putting their fingers to their lips. Faith was happy to see that Daniel wasn't upset by their cheeky mimicry.

"Dan! That's my name, too!" he said, as he heard Peter remonstrate with his sons.

Peter bore the two boys away to sit quietly in their pew and Daniel went to join Gavin and Bella. He had clearly recovered from the ordeal of the interrogation, and was back to his happy, easy-going self.

It was good to see a lot of new faces in the church today. There were people Faith suspected must have come from beyond Little Worthy, since she had never seen them before. But her own congregation were here in full force, too. Elsie Lively, a tiny old woman in an antiquated "best" hat with a bunch of fake cherries pinned to the side of it had just come into the porch. *Our church is alive and well,* Faith thought.

Elsie was now making her way towards Faith, carrying a tissue-wrapped package under her arm.

"Elsie! Welcome!" Faith reached out and clasped the woman's frail hands in hers. "How wonderful to see you. Are you looking forward to today?"

Elsie Lively was one of the oldest of Faith's parishioners, and – as her piece in the booklet proved – her family was probably the most old-established in Little Worthy. Elsie herself, before she retired, had spent all her working life behind the counter of the village post office.

"Yes, my dear, I certainly am," Elsie said, fumbling with the package as she took it out from under her arm to give to Faith. "It's a very special day for us at St James's. I've been working on a gift for our church. I'm not much of an artist, as I'm sure you'll see, but I've done my best."

"Oh, Elsie!" Faith unfolded the tissue paper to reveal a white linen altar cloth, embroidered with a large gold cross. Around the edge was a frieze of delicate cockleshells. "I had no idea you were working on something like this. It's incredible!"

The old altar cloth, which Faith had inherited when she took over as vicar of St James's, was beginning to fray in a couple of places, and there were a couple of marks on it that – even with the help of the very latest stain-removal products – she hadn't been able to completely eradicate.

The cherries on Elsie's hat quivered. "Why, thank you, dear. I've tried to do something similar to the old design, but I added the shells, you know, for St James."

"They're perfect!" Faith said. "And you definitely are an artist. All those years in the sewing group have certainly paid off!"

As she stroked one of the silken cockleshells with a fingertip, Faith felt something click into place in her mind and it left her skin cold. She excused herself to Elsie and made her way towards the calm of the vestry.

Laying the cloth aside in a drawer, she laid a hand against the steady stone of the wall. *Elsie's informal Monday night sewing group! Doesn't Pat make a point of turning up there every week?*

Faith knew she did. And if Pat was there, she could hardly have spent the entire evening with Jeremy as well. But perhaps Faith was getting ahead of herself. Her suspicions were unfair and unfounded.

Emerging once more, she saw the church was almost full now. In a couple of moments she would have to begin the service. By chance, Elsie was seated on a row of seats near to the vestry door. Faith edged to her side, leaned close and spoke quickly.

"Your sewing group, Elsie. Did you meet last Monday? Was Pat there?"

"Of course she was!" Elsie chirped. "Dear Pat. She helped me finish off the last couple of shells. Why?"

"Oh… no reason," said Faith, feeling distinctly troubled. "I suppose I should thank her too, then."

She glanced across to the porch, where the stout churchwarden was ushering the last family past her trestle table. So the alibi Pat had provided for Jeremy was false. *She lied to the police. But why?*

The organist was taking his seat. He glanced round to check that she was ready for him to begin playing a short piece to introduce the service. Faith nodded. Confronting Pat would have to wait. She made her way to the pulpit.

Faith's sermon – using some of the material from her foreword to the booklet – went down very well, and Peter and his wife were the first of many to come up and congratulate her afterwards.

"Loved it," Peter said. "Really brought it home that the spiritual side of things – well – not a soft option, is it?"

Sandy, Peter's wife, agreed. She grinned at Faith. "You made parts of the pilgrimage sound quite amusing, but how you survived without your make-up I can't imagine!"

"All part of the journey," Faith replied.

Dan and Charlie were tugging at their parents' hands, and she suggested that Peter and Sandy might like to take them over to the vicarage garden where they could explore the different stalls and perhaps find a bite to eat, as well.

"Faith, that was such an amazing sermon." Bella Wythenshaw was there, now. Her eyes were shining. She, too, seemed to have forgotten all about the police interrogation. "And I have to thank you for those wonderful old ropes. So kind of you to let us re-use them…"

"You should see what she's done," Gavin interrupted. "Woven them all around the top of the four-poster. Very arty indeed. Much nicer that those old cords and tassels that were up there before. Looks fantastic, love." He put his arm around his wife and pulled her into a close hug.

A slight commotion was occurring in the porch, and Faith went over to see what was going on. People were crowding around a tall, fair woman with stooped shoulders who had just come in. Gwen Summerly!

The watercolourist blinked nervously as she backed away from the flurry of questions and compliments that were being aimed at her.

"You've got the church off to a T," a woman in a blue suit and a pink straw hat, whom Faith didn't recognize, was saying. "And the flowers and everything are so pretty. We'd love you to do something similar for our dining room. Promise me you'll be able to do it!"

"Well – yes. I suppose I could." Gwen's voice was very soft. There was something passive about the droop of her shoulders, as she turned her face away from yet another effusive compliment.

It was impossible to conceive of Gwen committing an act of violence against Sal, however much she had disliked her. She was just too gentle. Too weak in manner and physicality.

Faith glanced over to the niche where Sal's painting rested, stark and sombre against the old stones of the wall. No one was looking at it. Someone plucked at Faith's sleeve.

"Sorry to bother you." It was Ethan, the young man from The Reaches. "Would it be OK if we started setting up some of our stuff?"

"Of course," Faith told him. "Go ahead. Everyone's really looking forward to your gig. Just make sure that you keep everyone out of the aisles until you've managed to tape down all the cables. OK?"

"Sure." Ethan nodded.

It was a shame that Fred wasn't around, being still laid up at home with his bad back. He'd have done a great job of making sure that everything was put up with care and an eye for safety. But Ethan seemed a very responsible person, and Pat would no doubt be hovering throughout the set-up.

Faith would have liked to take Pat aside, now that the service was over, and speak to her about what she had been up to on Monday night. Why she had told a blatant lie. But the church was still quite crowded, and the churchwarden was busy at her trestle table, handing out pamphlets and chatting to some new arrivals. It would be good to take a short break, and go over to Fred's cottage with some Free Foods cake. He'd be feeling a bit miserable at being excluded from everything, and a visit might cheer him up.

"Without you, I am nothing," Anya sang, the silvery notes soaring above the click of the drums and the driving energy of the guitar. *"With you, my life begins…"*

A love song, poignant and heartfelt – but a love song to Christ. The music came to an end, and a ripple of applause went up. There were even a few cheers and whoops from the younger members of the audience.

Out of the corner of her eye, Faith saw two people coming up the path to the church. An odd couple: an elderly woman with a mane of long grey hair leaning on the arm of a much younger man. Not members of her congregation – or indeed locals.

Pat seemed to be taking a break from her duties in the porch. Faith turned away from the concert and followed the couple into the church. Any newcomers to St James's must be made to feel especially welcome on this day of celebration.

She found the couple standing in front of Sal Hinkley's painting. The old woman was gazing up at it. She started when Faith spoke to her, and looked round with moist eyes.

"I'm so sorry, vicar," she said, looking at Faith's clerical garb. "I hope I'm not intruding. We're not – church people, I'm afraid. I can't remember the last time I stepped inside a church."

"Well, please don't apologize. We're very happy to see you at St James's – especially today. I don't think we've met, have we?"

The woman shook her head. "I'm Verity. Verity Goldman. This is my son, Gerald. We came because of Sal."

"Really?" Faith's curiosity was piqued. This was probably the first time today that anyone had paid much attention to Sal's painting. "You know the artist's work?"

"You could say that," Verity said. "You see, I taught Sal at art school. She was extraordinary. Such confidence, such vision, even in her first year. I knew she would go on to do great things… Oh, I suppose that sounds rather flippant in the circumstances."

Faith laid a hand on her arm. "Not at all, Ms Goldman. I know what you mean."

The old lady turned back to the painting and gazed at it in silence. Then she fumbled in her handbag and pulled out a tissue to wipe her eyes.

"Let's take a seat, Mum," said Gerald. He steered her to a pew where they could sit down. "I'll find us a cool drink," he added.

As Gerald headed off outside in search of some refreshments, Faith took a seat beside his mother.

"What was Sal like as a person, when you knew her?" Faith asked.

"Oh, quite a handful! As very talented people often are." Verity smiled and pulled a large, creased brown envelope out of her bag. She extracted a photograph from it. "Here we are. Winchester Art School, class of '83."

Faith stared at the group photograph. On the right-hand side, an elegant woman in a long, patterned dress with dark hair piled up on top of her head stood a little apart from the others. This was clearly Verity in her younger years. And it was impossible to miss Sal. Her slight figure stood right in the front of the line-up of colourful young men and women, staring at the camera with a fierce, unblinking gaze.

In the row behind, Faith noticed another familiar face, slightly plump and framed in straight fair hair. She gave a sharp intake of breath.

"Is that Gwen Summerly?" she asked. "I didn't realize she and Sal knew each other back then."

"Oh yes. They were quite good friends, initially," Verity said. "But they fell out over a chap. Him, to be precise. David." She indicated a tall youth with a lot of curly dark hair, who was standing beside Gwen.

"David McGarran?" Faith's skin tingled.

"That's right," Verity said. "A nice enough chap, and rather dashing-looking if I remember rightly, though his paintings would never have set the world on fire. He and Gwen were rather well suited, I thought. But the art school environment is a bit of a hothouse. By the second year he was running round after Sal, and poor Gwen was left quite out in the cold."

"That's sad," Faith said. It was easy to see how Gwen might have lost out. Her lack of assertiveness would have given her no advantage, if the fiery Sal were determined to have David. "Did you know that they married, Sal and David? It didn't last very long, though."

Verity shook her head. "I'm not at all surprised to hear that. Sal had so many admirers. That quality of wildness in a girl – it can be very compelling. Most of the lads were after her when she was at the art school, and one or two of the girls, too."

"And did she – reciprocate?" Faith asked.

"Oh, I really don't know. Probably. Of course, it was none of my business, her private life – and certainly not my place to

judge. I was just there to teach her. But she was extremely…
flighty – if you know what I mean."

As she heard this, Faith felt a strange conflict of emotion.
No doubt Sal's "flighty" behaviour would have caused a great
deal of heartbreak and confusion – not least to Gwen. But at
the same time, this vision into Sal's past, so intense and so
vivid, made the extinction of her life seem almost more tragic.

The porch door swung open and a line of Anya's vocals
drifted in. "*My life is to love you… What more could I ask?*"

Faith looked up into the roof vault, at the fine old timbers,
and tried to still a sudden shiver that was running through her
limbs. It was a great relief to see Verity's son Gerald approaching
with a tray of tea and cake.

CHAPTER

15

The sun had begun to drop in the sky as Faith stepped out of the porch. It was very quiet and warm in the churchyard. The band were taking a break among the gravestones, sipping water from paper cups. Under the largest yew tree she spotted Brian, looked rather overdressed in a fashionably crumpled cream linen suit. Ruth was beside him, exquisite in a short white skirt and a lacy *eau de nil* top with long, flared sleeves. Faith went over to join them.

"Hello, Big Sis. Where's Mum? Did she come with you after all?"

"Of course." Ruth gave her a sharp look. This was clearly not a "Big Sis" moment. "Mother's gone to look round the new garden."

"On her own?" Faith asked.

Brian cleared his throat. Faith found herself tensing in anticipation of one of his jocular "vicar" comments, but instead he said: "She's found herself a beau, Faith. Lovely old geezer with a walking stick. Plenty of go in the old girl, eh?"

"Bri!" Ruth slapped his arm playfully. "He seems a nice man, Faith. I've met him before when I've come over here. Isn't he one of your churchwardens?"

"Oh, yes." So Fred must have been feeling better. He'd be so glad to have made it over here. He'd have hated to miss the whole day. "Well – Mum will be in very good hands with him. Fred knows everything there is to know about the garden. He even planted most of the new trees himself."

"Right up Mother's street," Ruth said, shifting from foot to foot. She looked rather drawn and tired. Perhaps her feet were hurting. High-heeled grey slingbacks were not the best choice for standing around in a churchyard.

"Would you like to sit down, Ruth?" Faith asked. "There's plenty of free seats inside. Or I could bring you out a chair if you'd prefer."

Ruth shook her head, looking irritable. Faith wondered if perhaps things with Brian weren't going so well after all.

"That Georgian vicarage of yours is quite a pile, isn't it?" Brian said, suddenly, turning to Faith. "Way too big for one solitary lady. Massive garden, too. Though it looks like it could do with a bit of TLC."

Faith bristled. Had he given up his career in IT to become an estate agent? She noticed that her sister's shoulders had tightened a little, and her mouth was pulling down at the corners.

"If you were at the vicarage you must have seen the Free Foods stall," said Faith, trying the change to subject. "Did you try any of their food?"

"Certainly did. Cornish pasty. Scrumptious." Brian's dimple flashed. "Sorry – how rude of me, Faith. Can I get you something? You must be parched, with all the running around you've done today. Pretty good show, I must say. I like the music."

"You've done really well, Faith," Ruth said, managing a smile at last. She turned to Brian. "I don't know about my sister, but I'd love a nice chilled juice, Bri. Would you mind?"

"Of course, honey." Brian dropped a kiss on the top of Ruth's head and set off towards the mini-marquee in the vicarage garden.

"You don't like him, do you, Faith?" Ruth said, as soon as he was out of earshot. "It's written all over your face."

Faith hesitated, trying to choose the right words. Her back was aching and her throat was dry. Now that the day was almost over, now that she had stopped rushing around, she realized that she was very tired. "I'm just worried for you," she said. "But I'll admit, I find his manner a little trying sometimes."

Ruth sighed. "He's a good person, under all that bluster. Do you really think that I'd let him back into my life if he weren't? He made a stupid mistake, and he deeply regrets it."

"Are you sure?" Faith asked.

"Yes, really." Ruth gave Faith a long, steady look. "And what he said, just now, about the vicarage… He was trying to – help me out. Get the ball rolling…"

"What on earth are you talking about?"

"Faith. We *have* to talk about Mother."

"Now?"

"Yes. It's at the point of no return, Faith. And there's never a good time, is there?" Ruth straightened, standing tall as she faced Faith. "It's been lovely, having her to stay. But I won't tell a lie; it's also been extremely hard work. The house is too small for the three of us. Brian and I have had no privacy to speak of these last couple of days. Mother's forgetful, she leaves things lying around, and then she's always wandering about, back and forth, in and out of the living room, looking for them. She gets up in the night, thinking it's the morning. She's constantly under my feet in the kitchen. Nothing major, Faith, but very difficult in a tiny house. And – we looked at your vicarage, and the huge garden – and I thought back to last Christmas and how great it was, all of us sitting around the table in that great big kitchen of yours…"

It all became clear. Faith could have kicked herself. How could she not have seen this before? "Ruth, why didn't you say something?"

Her sister lowered her eyes. "I know how busy you are," she said.

"She's my *mother!*" said Faith. Her sister smiled thinly, in a way that only made Faith feel worse. Had she really given the impression that she was too embroiled in matters of the church to care for her own family? Perhaps she had…

"She would be much happier with you." Ruth's face looked suddenly bleak. "She's always liked you best."

"That's nonsense!" Faith countered, even though she saw the grain of truth. Her mother had certainly always seemed more comfortable in Faith's presence. There had been none of the teenage animosity that her sister had gone through.

Ruth reached out and gripped Faith's hand. "We're too alike, Mother and I. We wind each other up. You've got more of Dad in you."

A high-pitched squeal of feedback from the podium signalled that The Reaches were about to launch into the second half of their performance.

"Ruth. Mum adores you," said Faith. "But listen – we mustn't talk about all this now. Next week, when this is all over and Mum's back in Birmingham, let's get together. It's true I've got a lot of space…"

"Is it two spare bedrooms?"

"It's three, actually. Ridiculous, I know, for just one person. Listen, I'm not sure how it would work at the moment, but…" She stopped herself. It was true her responsibilities were manifold. Every day involved her going somewhere or other in the area. But her sister's life was no less hectic, she suspected. "We'll talk about it later," she said. Part of her wasn't really sure they'd reached this juncture yet. Their mother was so independent. Surely she'd be better off in her own place? If she sold her house, they could find a little flat for her in Winchester.

Ruth said nothing. She was staring down at the dry earth of the churchyard, her eyes very bright.

"I can't do it all on my own," she said, in a small voice.

Faith suddenly found her own eyes stinging. This was unheard of. Roo, vulnerable! Her "big" sister, so capable, so confident, always – never giving up, even when Brian left her.

Ethan leapt up onto the podium and struck a powerful chord on the guitar. It was his turn to sing now, a raucous, rough number about life on the city streets, while Anya accompanied him on a keyboard.

"*Thought I was alone,*" he sang. "*Lost in the crowd, sinking down so deep, so far…*"

"Let's go and find Mum," Faith said. "I'd like to know what she's been up to with Fred."

By the time Ruth, Brian and Marianne drove back to Winchester, the sun had set. The sky was turning a velvety shade of pinkish lavender as Faith strolled back from the lychgate to the church

– there was still plenty of light, but not for much longer. The Reaches had finished their set and were hurrying up and down the path, carrying their equipment to their battered old van. A few people still lingered in the churchyard, chatting and wandering around to peer at the gravestones.

Pat was standing just outside the porch. The trestle table had been folded away, and she was fussing with the last two boxes of leaflets. And, tired as she was, there was something that Faith must address.

"Have you got a moment, Pat?"

Pat flustered around, dragging one of the boxes towards the door. "I must get the last of these leaflets inside," she said. "There wasn't room for all of them in the porch, earlier. But now the dew will be falling. They could be *rrrr*uined."

"I'll help you, in just a moment. But there's something we need to talk through first."

"Surely it can wait?"

"It's about Jeremy, Pat."

With great reluctance the churchwarden ceased her efforts to drag the heavy box inside.

"I see," she said in a low voice, her eyes fixed on the toes of her white court shoes.

The two of them walked in silence to the commemorative garden. Most of the children had been taken home to bed now, and there were just a handful of people wandering about and admiring the new trees. Fred was holding court at the entrance to the arbour, sitting on one of the new benches. He waved his walking stick in greeting as Faith and Pat walked by.

The two of them went to the furthest corner of the arbour, where Percy Cartwright's bronze pony had been set up. The evening light picked up hints of reddish gold over its sleek metal body.

Pat squared her shoulders and stared at Faith defiantly. "Well – fire away," she said.

Faith looked around to check they were indeed enjoying some privacy. "Jeremy wasn't with you on Monday evening, was he?" she said. "The evening that Sal Hinkley died. He couldn't have been, because you were with Elsie Lively, helping her to finish off the altar cloth at the sewing club."

A flush spread across Pat's cheeks. "You've been checking up on me," she said meekly.

"What's going on?" said Faith. "Why did you lie to the police, Pat?"

Pat tossed a furtive glance over her shoulder, checking that no one was in earshot.

"You have no right to quiz me like this, Faith. Especially as Jeremy had absolutely nothing to do with Sal's death," she whispered.

Faith pressed on. "If you're convinced he's not guilty, why d'you feel the need to provide him with an alibi?"

Pat's cheeks flushed a dull scarlet. "It's a personal matter," she said. "Jeremy asked me to put in a good word for him, and I felt duty bound."

"*A good word?*" said Faith. "You *lied* to the police, Pat. If you want this to remain private, and not end up giving your explanations in court, you'd better tell me what's going on." The words came out more harshly than she intended, but *really*, Pat seemed unable to grasp the gravity of the situation.

"Look – Faith," said Pat. 'This is so difficult. Jeremy didn't want anybody to know where he was because he was with Gwen Summerly…"

Pat looked at her frankly, and it took a few moment for her meaning to dawn. "*With* Gwen Summerly?" said Faith. "You mean, *with* with?"

Pat's blush deepened as she bowed her head in assent. "That's correct. Romantically with. They're courting."

Faith blew out her cheeks. Well, that was a surprise.

"I suppose at least that provides an explanation for Jeremy's vociferous support of Gwen's watercolour," Faith said. "But you've been very naïve, getting drawn into all of this. I hope you're aware, Pat, that lying to the police is a very serious offence indeed."

Pat bridled. "I don't know what you mean, I'm sure," she snorted. "I may have told a small untruth about Jeremy's whereabouts, but I meant absolutely no harm by it. It was done with the best of intentions."

Faith was sorely tempted to say "*Try telling that to Inspector Shorter!*" but she stopped herself just in time.

Now, isn't this a tricky one, she thought. Ben should, of course, be informed of this new development – the liaison between Jeremy and Gwen – but she couldn't face speaking to him tonight. Tomorrow would be soon enough. She looked at Pat, whose sense of defiance seemed to be wilting by the second.

She really had gone the extra mile today, meeting and greeting all the visitors to the church. She'd given her all. It would be very tough on her to have to face another interrogation right now – and there was little doubt that Ben would have much sympathy. The niceties of "it was done with the best intentions" would cut no mustard with him.

"Pat, you've put me in a very difficult position here," said Faith. "I really don't know what to do for the best."

Pat blinked. "Well – whatever you must do, you must do, I suppose. But I must stress that I squared everything with my conscience. My motives were impeccable."

There was nothing more to be said. Faith left Pat in the garden and headed back to the churchyard. She called out a greeting to Farrah and Jasper as she passed the Free Foods stall.

"How did it go? Have you had a good day?"

"Brilliant!" Jasper replied. "We've sold out of just about everything. Three Bakewell tarts and a couple of Cornish pasties left, and that's it. The takeaway gazpacho was a huge success."

"It was quite delicious," Faith said. "Perfect for a hot day – it rather reminded me of my time in Spain."

"I didn't know you'd been to Spain," Farrah said.

"Ah – of course, you missed my sermon this morning. Never mind. You can catch up with the story in our pamphlet. There's still a few going spare."

Faith suggested that the two of them could shut up shop if they wanted to, and head for home. The local hotdog van was due to arrive on the Green very soon, and would cater for any latecomers who were hungry.

"But why don't I buy those last tarts and the pasties – the youngsters in the group will probably appreciate them when they've finished packing up."

Jasper placed all the leftover eatables in a box, and despite Faith's protestations, supplied them for free. Faith carried it over to the van and gave it to Ethan. He thanked her, and ran back up to the church to share the goodies with the others. Faith was just following him up the path, at a weary snail's pace, thinking – *at last, I can stop!* – when the lychgate creaked behind her.

"Faith Morgan?" said a man's firm voice.

Faith stopped in her tracks. Patrick Mills, the gallery owner, was bearing down on her with a black briefcase in his hand. It was quite discomfiting, surreal even, seeing him so far from his natural environs. Like a strange creature. What had possessed him to turn up at this late hour?

His heavy footsteps crunched up the path and came to a halt beside Faith. He eyed The Reaches, sitting on their podium munching the Cornish pasties – Ethan with a guitar at his feet – with mild disapproval.

"What's this, then? The happy-clappy brigade?"

"Can I help you?" Faith asked.

"Apologies – that came across wrongly," Mills said, his thick brows pulled down low. "Frightfully rude of me, of course. I've actually come on rather a delicate matter – to collect Sal's painting."

"Oh?" said Faith, struggling to understand. "You mean the one of the church? Can I ask what you want it for?"

Mills flashed her an unnerving and slightly smug smile. "Why, to add to the sale, of course."

Faith frowned. "The painting belongs to the church, surely. It's inside at the moment."

Mills's smile vanished. "Oh, but I must correct you there," Patrick said. "The painting is listed in the catalogue for tomorrow's sale. Any prospective purchasers must be able to view it before they bid. It'll go for a considerable amount, I imagine, but no one will buy it unseen."

It was as if he had thrown a bucket of icy water over her head. Faith stood on the path with her mouth open.

"You might like to check the situation with your colleagues on the parochial council," Mills said, his face relaxing into a rather oily smile. "It was all very clearly laid down when Sal undertook the commission."

"I'm sure you're right," said Faith. Mills might be unpalatable in some respects, but she didn't get the feeling he was dishonest. "But do you mind if I make a call to check?"

Mills made a show of checking his watch. "Go ahead," he said, "but can we make it quick?"

Faith pulled out her mobile. There was one person who would definitely be able to clear this matter up – Jeremy Taylor.

"Here you are, Faith," Jeremy said, brandishing a handful of paperwork as he strode into the porch. He'd come straight from his house, striding over the field, as the last of the fete's guests departed for the day. Only Fred remained, and he was wandering on his own, slightly stiffly, in the arbour. "I've looked through the contract for the commission," said Jeremy. "We at St James's merely purchased the right to reproduce the painting. The original artwork belongs, of course, to the deceased Ms Hinkley's estate. Check it, if you don't believe me."

"There's no need," Faith said. A bleak tide of disappointment swamped her. Patrick Mills was already donning a pair of gloves to pick up the painting from its stand.

"Thank you, Mr Taylor," he said.

"I must say, I'll be sorry to see it go," said Faith.

Neither man responded.

Faith followed Mills out to his navy blue Audi estate car and watched as he loaded Sal's painting carefully into the boot, folding bubble wrap neatly around the edges and taping it up. Once the job was done, he turned to her and spoke much more affably.

"It'll go to a good home," he said. "An art lover's home."

"I'm sure," said Faith, wondering what he was implying.

Mills opened his briefcase on the bonnet of the car, and passed a thick, glossy catalogue to Faith. "This is the brochure for the sale, should you wish to pop along. You'll see the painting is listed at the end." He must have known there was little possibility she would be able to get to London at such short notice.

Still, Faith leafed through, and saw the appropriate entry on the last page. *A South-facing View of St Francis's Church – Little Worthy, Hampshire.*

St Francis's Church? Faith felt a rush of irritability. Was St James's really of so little importance to Sal that she didn't bother to check that she had the right saint when she titled the painting? It was as if even from beyond the grave she couldn't help but give offence.

"I should be going, then," Mills said. "Thank you for being so accommodating."

Faith pulled herself together and stood up. She was being uncharitable. Exhaustion was pulling her off balance. Religion had meant nothing to Sal. Saints names would have had no significance for her.

"I'm so sorry for the confusion," she said. "There's just one thing, Mr Mills. The catalogue gives the title as 'St Francis's Church'. But it's actually St James's. Sal must have got it wrong. Would you be able to change it? It's rather a major inaccuracy."

Mills laughed. "Typical Sal!" he said. "Don't worry, I'll get a correction slip printed, and I'll make sure that the auctioneer is aware." He shook Faith's hand and eased himself into the driving seat, then closed the door with the window down. His plump face held a reflective expression. "Sal was hopeless, you know. Couldn't organize her way out of a paper bag, if you know what I mean. I always told her what to do, every step of the way. Even to the extent of sorting the legal stuff for the divorce."

"I didn't know you and she went that far back," said Faith. Mills looked puzzled. "Eh?"

"You helped her with her divorce," Faith said, "from David McGarran."

"Yes, but that was only in the last three months," said Mills. "Can you believe it – thirty years apart from that McGarran fellow – and neither one of them had bothered with a legal separation?"

It was Faith's turn to frown. Hadn't Pat called Sal a divorcee from the start? Could she have been mistaken? And why hadn't McGarran mentioned it? He'd said that Sal had come to see him recently but he didn't mention anything about divorce proceedings.

Mills turned his key in the ignition and drove away.

Faith looked back to the church and saw Jeremy still waiting at the porch. He gave her a wave. "All hunky-dory?" he called. "If so, I'll head on home."

Faith's resolve hardened suddenly. "Actually, would you wait just a moment?" she said. "I'd like to speak to you." Jeremy looked rather startled at her tone. *No bad thing, given what I have to say!* she thought. Then she brushed Jeremy's elbow with her hand, steering him onto the far side of one of the yew trees, away from any prying eyes.

"I've really got a lot to be getting on with," he said, with a disapproving sniff.

"It's about Pat," said Faith, then waited for the words to sink in. "You asked her to lie on your behalf, Jeremy, by providing you with a false alibi when you were actually spending time with Gwen Summerly. It's not for me to question your morality," she said, "but when your untruths draw in a dear member of my congregation, I feel I must speak out."

Jeremy's jawline tightened. "I resent this intrusion into my private life," he muttered. "It's none of your business."

"I agree. I would much rather know nothing about your personal situation. But Pat is my churchwarden, and anything that concerns her – especially if it might lead her into serious trouble – is most definitely my business. She's a good woman, Jeremy, and she deserves better than to be dragged into this."

"How dare you!" Jeremy kept his voice low, but he leaned his thin face close to Faith, mouthing the words with great exaggeration. "You're trying to blackmail me. You should be ashamed of yourself, vicar."

Faith shook her head. "I'm simply trying to protect Pat from becoming involved in something that might be very detrimental to her. And I'm asking you, Jeremy, how it can possibly be right to ask her to lie for you? It's a serious offence to withhold information from the police. If you wish to do that, then that's your choice and you may pay the price. But to involve another, innocent party…"

"Gah!" Jeremy spat a wordless exclamation of frustration at Faith. "You're twisting this whole thing right out of proportion. I merely wished for a little privacy, that's all. But I have nothing to hide. Absolutely nothing." He pulled his mobile out of his pocket and dialled a number. "Is that the police headquarters? I'd like to be put through to Detective Inspector Shorter, please. Yes, it's rather urgent. And I will only speak to the DI himself. Thank you."

Jeremy marched off across the churchyard, the phone pressed close to his ear. Faith felt an odd sense of deflation rather than triumph as she half-heard the stilted conversation that followed. There was really little satisfaction in hearing Jeremy Taylor grilled from the other end of the phone. Her mood lifted, though, when she saw Fred limping on his stick towards her.

"What a wonderful day!" he said. "Everyone so happy, and the garden looking so good. Wouldn't have missed it, not for the world."

"You're a wonder, Fred," Faith told him. "Thank you so much for looking after my mother. She said you were so interesting to talk to – such an expert."

A smile dawned on Fred's face. "She's a lovely lady. She knows her plants, too. A pleasure to talk to her. But Faith, you should see the arbour, on its first official day of existence," he said. "We'll just make it, before the light goes." He held his arm out to her in an inviting crook.

"Will your back hold up?"

"It's getting better by the minute," Fred said, taking her arm as they headed, very slowly, back towards the arbour.

CHAPTER

16

They found Pat seated on a bench on the edge of the garden, looking into her lap. At their approach her face brightened, though clearly with some effort.

Faith offered her a wholehearted smile. "Hello, Pat," she said. *Perhaps at last she's realizing how misguided her actions were.* She only hoped Ben went easier on her after Jeremy revealed her deception.

"Hello, you two," said the churchwarden.

Fred lowered himself gingerly beside her, and gestured with his stick towards the sculpture of Eligius. "Well – that's a beautiful thing," Fred said. "Who'd have thought old Percy could come up with something like that?"

"Of course, it used to be Andrea's pony," Pat explained. "So I suppose he would have had plenty of time to study it. Did you know, Fred – she gave the animal to the local riding school? I saw Percy leading it along the road to the stables with all its tackle on. The saddle, and everything. So expensive, all that horse gear. Must have cost a fortune. And she just gave it all away. I expect the pony was worth a fair bit, too."

"They're good, generous people, the Cartwrights," Faith said. "No doubt about that. We'll miss them."

Fred nodded. "Good people are our speciality in Little Worthy. So kind of Gavin Wythenshaw, to put those trees in for me."

The sun had dipped, but the air was still warm. "Would you like to come back to the vicarage?" asked Faith. "We could have a restorative cup of tea – celebrate a fantastic day."

"Very nice," Fred said.

"Well, I don't know," Pat said, with a sidelong glance at Faith. She seemed unsure of her welcome at the vicarage. "It's very late."

"Do come, Pat," she said. "You've been an absolute brick today."

The evening was very still as they strolled out of the garden, making their way to the vicarage.

"Faith – listen!" Pat grabbed her arm as they went through into the kitchen. "What's that?"

The shrill whoop of a siren was going off. Not something that was often heard, on a Sunday evening in Little Worthy.

"It's the police," Pat gasped, her hand shaking. "Oh, Faith – what can it mean? What's happened now?"

Faith recognized the sound. But it wasn't the manic shriek of a police vehicle. It was a slow, mournful wail. Her heart quickened.

"It's an ambulance, Pat. Not the police."

Pat's thin eyebrows shot up. "An ambulance? Oh dear."

The siren was growing louder, speeding nearer to the centre of the village with every second.

Faith thought with a chill of fear of all the elderly people that lived in and around Little Worthy. Perhaps one of them had suffered a heart attack or a stroke... *Let it not be so,* she prayed. *Let this day of celebration end in joy...*

Ten seconds later, the ambulance swished past the vicarage gate, and headed off towards the other side of Little Worthy.

"Let's go in," Faith said. "There's nothing we can do, if it's a medical emergency. And if we're needed, everyone knows where to find us. I think we could all do with some tea."

Pat's phone – a plain, silver handset from the days before smartphones came on the scene – began warbling as they went through into the kitchen. Pat's florid face turned very pale as she took the call.

"I'm so sorry to hear that," she said into the handset, choking slightly. "That's terrible. Yes, yes, of course. I'll tell Faith. I'm with her now, at the vicarage. I'll let her know."

She put the phone away, shaking her head slowly.

"Who is it?" Fred asked, biting his lip.

"Elsie. Elsie Lively," Pat replied, her little eyes sombre.

"Elsie?" Faith's heart turned to ice. Dear Elsie, so frail, yet such an indomitable member of the St James's congregation. Elsie, who had toiled for months with her arthritic fingers to embroider the exquisite new altar cloth...

Fred clapped a hand over his eyes. "Not our Elsie—"

"No, no, no!" Pat exclaimed, giving him a brusque tap on the arm. "Elsie's fine. That was her on the phone just now."

"Is it Grace?" Faith asked, thinking sadly of Elsie's older sister, a sweet-voiced, gentle old lady who rarely left the house now.

"*No!*" Pat was becoming very exasperated. "It's nothing to do with Grace. *If* the pair of you would just let me get a word in edgeways! It's Timothy Johnston's daughter. She's come off her pony. Right outside Elsie's cottage. Terrible. Absolutely terrible."

Faith caught her breath. She remembered having seen the grey pony leaping and prancing in the road watched nervously by Emily's father. It was clearly a high-spirited animal. But Emily had seemed so relaxed, so confident, up there in the saddle.

Fred's face was creased with anxiety. "Is it bad?"

Pat was trembling a little. "Horses can kill you, even when they don't mean to. That young girl should never have taken him out on her own. It's not safe."

"Perhaps she wasn't on her own," Faith said, remembering how Emily's father had been so attentive, so careful with the lively pony. "Fred – will you be all right to hold the fort here while Pat and I go over and try to find out what happened? Brew some tea, if you feel up to it. We'll have it when we come back."

"I'll do that," Fred said. "It'll be a pleasure. Tell them…" he hesitated. "Tell them I'll be thinking of the little lass. Wishing her well."

"I will!" Faith hurried back to the front door with Pat. As they reached the vicarage gate, two police cars shot past, sirens blaring.

Just what exactly is going on? Faith wondered.

The lane outside Elsie's cottage had been rendered impassable by the ambulance and an accompanying police van. There were three officers in uniform, plus a substantial crowd of spectators, and at first Faith struggled to make sense of the scene. She noticed that a dark blue estate car had been run up onto the grassy bank on the opposite side of the lane. It rested there in a lopsided fashion, its hazard lights blinking.

"That's Patrick Mills's car," said Faith.

Pat wasn't listening. She grabbed Faith's arm, turning her in the other direction. "There's the culprit!"

Eligius was standing at the side of the lane, tied to a gate post. His neck was arched and he was watching all the activity with wide, rolling eyes. Every now and then he pawed at the tarmac with a front hoof, as if impatient to be released.

"I don't think we should jump to conclusions until we know what happened," Faith said. "The accident may not have been the pony's fault."

There was a flurry of activity in the lane, and someone said, "Stand back, please. We need to move her."

Faith craned her neck and caught a glimpse of Emily's slight body, lying flat and still under a red blanket. A green-clad paramedic was kneeling at her head, carefully positioning a plastic neck brace. The young girl was still wearing a helmet. Timothy stood back a little, his shoulders taut and his hands pressed to his forehead.

"Could you step back, sir?" asked the paramedic.

Timothy nodded, never taking his eyes from Emily. Faith noticed he wasn't wearing the thick gloves today, but there was a white bandage wound round the palm of his right hand. As Emily had a neck brace fitted, her father seemed to come round from his daze and stumbled past her, heading for the estate car.

"You idiot!" he shouted, waving the bandaged hand in the direction of the vehicle. "You came round that corner at fifty miles an hour! What the hell were you thinking of?"

Patrick Mills stepped out from behind the car, and stood beside a policeman. He was clutching a white handkerchief to his forehead, already stained with blood. "Look – I'm so sorry," he said. "I didn't see the horse until the last moment. I simply couldn't stop."

"You fool," Timothy yelled. "You utter, stupid, careless... fool!" His words degenerated into something like a sob.

"Daddeee!" a thin, high wail went up from Emily. She was struggling to sit up, but the paramedic placed a hand on each of her shoulders.

"Baby?" Timothy stumbled towards his daughter. "Baby, what is it?"

Faith edged herself closer through the gathered villagers, and heard Emily say, "I'm fine, Daddy. Please don't make a fuss. I'm all right."

"Just lie back, sweetheart," the paramedic said calmly. "We'll get you seen to at the hospital."

"Do as the man says," said Timothy. "Daddy will come with you in the ambulance."

"Timothy, are you all right?" Faith said, touching his arm. "Would you like me to come with you to the hospital?"

Timothy stared at her, his eyes wide. "Please, Faith. If you could. Clarisse – she's at home with our boy. She doesn't even know this has happened."

"I'll go there now," Pat said, stepping forward. "I'll sort some childcare out and then I'll drive Clarisse to the hospital, Timothy. You must be together at a time like this."

The paramedic's colleague wheeled over a stretcher, and the two of them began the delicate procedure of easing Emily onto it without jolting her spine.

The grey pony, as if sensing that he was about to abandoned, let out a strident whinny from the gate.

"Diamond!" Emily gasped. "He's frightened. He needs me!"

A young policewoman bent over her. "Don't worry, love," she said. "Does he live at the riding stables? I'll walk him back there when the ambulance has gone. He'll be fine. He's a lovely pony, isn't he?"

"He's the best pony ever," Emily whispered, as the stretcher was loaded into the ambulance.

Faith stepped inside the vehicle and sat next to Timothy. As the ambulance departed, swaying ponderously along the lane, she reached out and took his good hand in hers for a brief moment of reassurance.

"All will be well," she told him, devoutly hoping that it would indeed be so.

She wondered how he'd injured his hand. Now that the bandage was in plain sight, it would seem an obvious question to ask him, but Faith couldn't bring herself to do it.

Timothy had noticed her looking. "Rope burn," he said, looking back at Emily. "That pony can't half pull when he wants to."

"Of course," said Faith.

It was 10 p.m. and fully dark by the time Faith finally got back to the vicarage. A faint white mist hung over the lawn, and there was a slight chill in the air. *Midsummer is past*, she thought, a little sadly, remembering the bluish light that had lingered on the horizon even at midnight all through the previous weeks. St James's Day had come and gone. July was almost over. The earth was turning on its axis, and they were heading down to autumn.

The kitchen was deserted: Fred must have long since hobbled his way home, unless he had managed to cadge a lift from someone. A full teapot was waiting for Faith in the middle of the table. Despite the fact that Fred had wrapped it in a towel to keep the heat in, the pot and its contents were stone cold.

Faith put the kettle on, kicked off her shoes and sat at the kitchen table to mull over the events of the evening. Emily, much to everyone's relief, had sustained no serious injury. A CT scan had revealed no damage to her spine or internal organs. She had got off with just some bad bruises and a severe headache after her heavy fall on the tarmac. Because of the headache, the hospital in Winchester wanted to keep her overnight – just in case a concussion should develop. Timothy, all smiles now that he knew his beloved daughter was not in any danger, had insisted on settling down for the night in an armchair beside her bed.

Faith couldn't switch off. Her mind kept returning to the injury on Timothy's hand. A rope burn from the lead reins, he'd said. *And why shouldn't it be?*

But Peter – was it Peter? – had said that forensics believed Sal was strangled by some sort of cord.

Faith tried to shake the thought away. After all, what motive would Timothy have had to do harm to Sal Hinkley? He was a very committed Christian, with a strong sense of family values. He might have found some aspects of Sal's morality questionable. But there was no cause to be violent.

Faith felt her energy begin to drop as she lapsed into a huge yawn. She must just check her mobile, which she'd left behind when she rushed out with Pat after the ambulance. And then she could gulp down some hot tea and stagger up to bed. The mobile was lying there, right in front of her, on the bare wood of the kitchen table.

She picked it up and viewed the activity logs. Two voicemails were waiting for her, both from Ben. And a text, also from him. *CALL ME, ASAP!* He must have found out about Jeremy Taylor and Gwen Summerly. And he'd be furious with her for not sharing this startling new information with him. *Best get it over with!* Faith didn't wait to listen to the voicemails, but dialled his number straight away.

"Yup?" he grunted, picking up on the first ring.

The back of Faith's neck tingled with apprehension. He sounded very annoyed, but she tried to keep her cool.

"Hello, Ben. It's me. Faith."

"Where the hell've you been?"

"I'm sorry. I rushed out – and forgot my phone. It was a bit of an emergency. One of the local girls fell off her pony. I had to go with her and her father to the hospital."

Ben muttered something rather uncharitable about "*Florence Nightingale.*"

"The girl's fine, by the way. She's staying in hospital overnight, but she wasn't badly hurt," Faith said, a little tartly.

Ben made no apology. "I've been waiting to speak to you for two hours, Fay. There's been some *developments.*"

"I know. I'm sorry, I was going to speak to you in the morning about this." *Here it comes…*

There was a silence on the other end of the call. Then Ben said, gruffly, "So *you've* spoken to Sal Hinkley's solicitor, too?"

"Sal's solicitor?" Faith's head felt full of cotton wool. Why was it that Ben always seemed to confront her with insoluble puzzles when she was simply too tired to make sense of anything?

"Yup. He called me this evening. Came into headquarters and we had a very interesting chat. On the back of which I have now reopened the investigation into David McGarran."

"Oh," said Faith. *He's found out about the divorce, then.* But was that really enough to tip McGarran over the edge? Mills had made it sound like a formality.

"Is that all you have to say?" said Ben.

"Is this to do with the divorce?" asked Faith.

"It certainly is," said Ben. "Mr McGarran neglected to inform us of his full marital status at his first interview. When I say *neglected*, I mean, of course, *lied*."

"He told me that he and Sal met just once," said Faith. "A few days ago. All very amicable. But why kill her, Ben? It sounds like the divorce was a formality."

Ben laughed. "That's the thing, Faith – they *weren't* divorced. He never signed the papers."

"Ah," said Faith. She was struggling to keep up.

"Ah, indeed," said Ben. "So maybe McGarran has a motive after all."

"You're kidding," Faith said, as her vision of McGarran's sad face crystallized into something a little more sinister. She remembered the hiked-up prices in the sale catalogue for the auction – and the printed slip stating that they might well go much higher, now that the artist was deceased. "So if he's still in line to receive Sal's estate he could end up a very rich man?"

"*Exactly!*" said Ben. "Of course, he's whimpering on about being completely innocent. But what a motive, eh? It's a darned shame that without some more concrete evidence the chief won't let me hold him much longer."

Faith's mind was whirling. Was it really much of a motive? McGarran hadn't seen his wife for thirty years. In those three decades, Sal might have hooked up with someone else. She might have made a will – and left everything to that someone else. So wouldn't David McGarran be taking a bit of a gamble, killing her without being sure he was still her sole heir?

She shared this thought with Ben.

"You know what I think, Fay?" Ben's voice buzzed in her ear, an intimate sensation, in the semi-darkness of the kitchen. "It might have been the money he was after. But it could be a little more complicated. I think when Sal instigated the divorce proceedings, it kicked the guy over the edge. Either McGarran was desperate to get his hands on her loot, or it was some old emotional thing that he'd never resolved."

A slightly dismissive note had crept into his voice. Faith held the mobile a few inches from her ear, to distance herself from him. Why did Ben always have to be so derogatory about "feelings" – considering them purely as factors to be added up when assessing evidence?

She thought back to the strange hunger in McGarran's face as he attempted to cross the police tape and go to Sal's painting hut. Classic behaviour of the guilty party, Ben would say. The criminal obsessively returning to the scene of the crime... But was that really what it was? Or was it an echo of the old love, the old pain that he felt for his long-lost wife? A need to capture in his memory the place where she breathed her last?

A frisson of disappointment passed over Faith at the thought that McGarran, outwardly so affable, so believable, had been keeping the truth from her. It was a good performance, though. She'd felt so sorry for him, with his bad jokes and his nostalgia for the past... the way he wanted to visit the church again, harking back to his childhood. And could it all have been manipulation, so she'd think he was a harmless, soft-hearted romantic?

"Ben, I have a confession to make," she said, coming to a sudden decision. No use in dwelling too much on her subjective impressions of McGarran. Whatever his motivation and his actions were, Ben would dig down until he'd got the truth. And he was in a reasonably positive frame of mind now. A good time to come clean.

"What, another one?" Ben didn't sound impressed. "So what've you done this time? Accidentally made off with some of the takings at your church fete?"

"Don't be rude. This is important." She told him about Pat's cover-up of Jeremy Taylor's liaison with Gwen. "Don't persecute her about this, Ben. She's rather naïve. I've advised her what a serious offence it is, to withhold information like that. I don't think she fully realized what she was getting into."

"Well, well. The idiocy of some people never surprises me," Ben said. "But honestly, Fay. Do you really think I've got time to piddle around taking your old Pat Montesque to task? Life's too short."

"All right, Ben," she said. And though his tone galled, she thanked him for being so understanding.

"I'd better go, Ben," she added. "It's been a long day. I'm sure we both need a good night's sleep. I certainly do."

"Night then, Fay," Ben said, in a neutral tone, and cut the call before she had time to thank him for the dinner the day before.

Faith was too tired now even to make herself that cup of tea. The kettle had switched itself off long ago, and already the water was cooling. She got up from the table and stumbled up the stairs to the bedroom, half-hoping that the Beast might have decided to favour her with his presence tonight. The warm weight of his furry body against her back would be very comforting as she slept.

There was no sign of the cat in the silent bedroom. He must be outside somewhere, hunting for small rodents among the shrubs of the vicarage borders. A sliver of moon had risen outside, and was casting a block of silvery light over the bedcover. Faith lay down in her clothes and fell immediately asleep.

CHAPTER

17

On Monday morning, Faith woke with a depressing sense of anti-climax. The windows were open, but the air in the bedroom felt thick and humid; possibly even hotter than yesterday. She must have disrobed at some point in the night, because her clerical gown was horribly crumpled at the bottom of the bed. *Never mind. It should go to the cleaners anyway, after being worn all day yesterday.* She went to take a shower.

As she lowered the Venetian blinds in the bathroom to open the window, the thin string caught on her fingers as it rushed upwards, snagging and pulling tight, and she was suddenly transported back to a forensics lecture in her days at the police college. To a selection of belts, wires, electrical flexes, and even a "professional" SAS garrotte with two wooden handles, all laid out on a table. Murder weapons, all of them.

The lecturer – an elderly man with a crooked back (he was reputed to have been injured in a bank robbery shoot-out sometime back in the 1970s, when he was a serving officer) had picked up each item in turn, demonstrating the force needed for an effective killing, and – if one was not using the

SAS model – the care one would need to take not to damage one's hands in the process.

"Gloves would have to be worn," he'd said, demonstrating with a length of piano wire. "Or as your victim struggled – and believe me, they *do* struggle – you could lose a finger."

Faith detached her hand from the Venetian blind cord with a slight shiver. *Had Sal struggled? She must have done – once she realized what was happening to her.* She stepped into the shower cubicle under the hot water, trying to relax. But she found it almost impossible. Perhaps, until now, her mind had simply refused to comprehend the brutal horror of the killing. Peter had described what had been used to kill Sal as something akin to a woman's thin belt. But it was the lecturer's words about damaged hands that held her attention.

She'd had ample opportunity to observe Timothy Johnston's bandaged hand, yesterday evening at the hospital. From the way that he cradled it, every now and then, it seemed to be quite sore. And those gloves he'd been wearing, when he was leading Emily on the road… had he been taking some pains to conceal the injury, until his daughter's accident pushed everything except her safety from his mind? *I should have asked him about it*, Faith thought, while knowing for certain that she never would have. She was his vicar, not his interrogator.

Only now she was alone – now that there was no immediate demand for her to offer care and support to anyone – it was impossible to stop her mind running on in deductive mode.

But what possible motive could Timothy have? She disliked clichés, but the phrase "pillar of the community" could have been invented for him.

She was seeing gloves everywhere! Gavin Wythenshaw had a pair hanging from his back pocket as he ran so energetically up the spiral staircase into the belfry. He was a very fit man, wiry and muscular. Faith remembered the fearless, easy strength with which he had swung himself out across the void to inspect the ropes. If he had his gloves with him, Gavin would certainly have the capability to kill someone with a makeshift garrotte. Though if he had killed Sal, would he really have been able to remain so cheerful – so relaxed – with the scene of his crime just a few hundred yards away? Would he have not only hung the bell ropes, but offered to come back and plant the trees?

And now the principal suspect was David McGarran. Faith thought back to the day she had met him up by Sal's hut, and shown him around the church. There was something very soft and lax about David's shambling body. She could see Ben's angle, but it was such an unsubtle one. Did he really have the determination, the actual physical strength, to strangle his ex-wife? He worked with his hands making picture frames – but that was delicate work.

Faith grabbed a towel and rubbed her wet hair with it. Ben had been on a high last night, convinced that David McGarran was his man. It just didn't feel right to her. Aside from the questions of physical capability, he didn't strike her as a greedy man. The sort of man who would covet his ex-wife's money. He was a *picture-framer*, for goodness' sake, which surely wasn't a profession to go into if acquiring wealth was a priority.

But the other motive that Ben had spoken of – the emotional one? That might be more likely. Sal walked out on McGarran thirty years ago, and he'd never bothered to initiate a divorce. But that might not be due to apathy. Perhaps McGarran had hoped she might come back to him. She was impetuous – a creature of impulse – why wouldn't she turn up again one day? Maybe Sal's reappearance had reawakened in him a love that he'd thought was lost to him for ever – and so he'd refused her request for a divorce. Faith could imagine Sal saying particularly horrible things to rile him.

Faith gave herself a mental shake. She was becoming obsessive. And all this speculation was an indulgence for a woman who had long ago abandoned a career as a detective. As she ran a comb through her damp hair, she considered the prospect before her. Today was Monday, and she must step back into her normal routine as vicar of St James's. Beginning with some day-to-day admin over at the vestry (much of which had been neglected in the run-up to the anniversary) and continuing with her weekly visit to Cedars Lodge House, a residential care home just outside Little Worthy. The elderly inmates who were too infirm to join in the celebrations yesterday would be looking forward to hearing what had happened.

As Faith walked over to the church, a thin layer of cloud had built up, veiling the sun that had been blazing down for the last couple of weeks. Rather than lowering the temperature, this seemed to add an almost tropical intensity to the summer heat. A trail of paper cups, hot-dog wrappers and discarded booklets littered the gravel of the path in the churchyard. She stooped to gather them up for the recycling bin. It would be at least a few days before Fred's bad back recovered sufficiently for him to return to duty.

Once inside the church, she avoided looked at the niche where Sal's painting had rested, and headed straight for her desk in the vestry. The clipboard might be a thing of the past, but a new pile of paperwork was already building up for her attention. A very substantial bill for the new bell ropes lay on top of the pile. Faith sat down and switched her laptop on so she could pay it by direct transfer. It was done in a matter of moments and, setting the bill aside to be filed, she riffled through the rest of the pile.

A black-and-white photograph slid out from among the papers and tumbled onto the floor. Faith retrieved it. *The old forge – with Percy Cartwright's great-grandfather outside!* She had better drop it off to Percy and Andrea on her way over to Cedars Lodge. They'd be glad of this old family keepsake, in their new home in France.

Andrea Cartwright answered the door with an apron tied tightly at her waist, and a scarf covering her dark hair.

"Have I called at a bad moment?" Faith asked, holding out the envelope with the photo. "I just wanted to give this back to Percy."

"Goodness, no!" There was no mistaking the welcome in Andrea's smile. "Please, do come in. We're all at sixes and sevens – but I know you'll forgive the mess. Percy's just popped over to the estate agents. There's a couple of things to clear up before the sale can go through. They're rushing it through for us, you know – exchange and completion at the same time."

Faith looked round at the avalanche of boxes and crates that had invaded Andrea's normally very tidy living room.

"Are you taking all that with you to the new house?"

"No, no. We'll put it into storage, and go through it all at some time in the future. Percy's happy to bin the lot, since there's no one to inherit it – but I can't do it, Faith. There's so much stuff that's been in his family forever. Furniture, wonderful old books, pictures. It builds up when a house has been lived in for generations."

Faith held out the envelope. "Of course it does," she said. "And I think you're absolutely right not to get rid of it all. It would be a terrible shame to lose so much history."

Andrea took the photograph out and looked at it with a little sigh. "He looks so like Percy, doesn't he? All those generations of Cartwright men, so strong and doughty, working at the forge." She slipped it into the pocket of her apron. "I doubt Percy will even remember he gave it to you, but I'll keep it safe, don't worry."

Faith was just about to say goodbye when Andrea asked her if she'd like to sit down for a moment and have a cold drink.

"It's frightfully close today, don't you think? You must be thirsty."

Faith glanced at her watch. It was almost midday – she should really be on her way to Cedars Lodge by now. But she could probably get away with staying another fifteen minutes or so, and Andrea was insistent.

"Please stay! I've just made some lemonade. Percy and I will never use all of it. Come on through. We can sit out in the backyard. He put the umbrella up for me this morning."

Andrea headed off towards the kitchen at the back of the house, and Faith followed her. The hall had clearly not been packed up yet. There were coats hanging from a hatstand, and a medley of books and papers on a small table where the telephone rested. Lots of framed photographs on the walls, too. An aerial shot of the centre of Little Worthy – with the forge clearly shown. It must have been taken a while back, for in the photograph the colour of the grass on the Green had faded to a dull yellow. Next to it was a striking shot of a young man, auburn hair swept back off his high forehead. Faith paused.

There was something oddly familiar about the young man's chiselled cheekbones; something very compelling about the air of slight desperation with which he confronted her from the photograph.

"Who's this, Andrea?" she asked.

"Who's who?" Andrea was already in the kitchen. Faith heard glasses clinking, and a *thunk* as the fridge door opened.

"The boy in this photograph. With the auburn hair."

"Oh goodness." Andrea came back into the hall, wiping her hands on her apron. "Don't you know? That's Rory, Faith. Percy's son."

"Rory?" Faith studied his pale face. Perhaps it was the family likeness that had caught her attention. The strong bones, the wide mouth, and – now she saw it – the red hair. Percy's head might have long ago turned white, but his stubble told a story of a red-headed past.

"Do come through," Andrea said, turning away.

Faith had to stay a moment longer. There was something taut and reserved in Rory's expression. Eyes alive with intelligence. Did he have some premonition of what was going to happen to him? Or had he perhaps inherited a propensity towards melancholy from his father, as well as his striking good looks? She made her way through to the kitchen, and out of the back door to where Andrea was sitting at a teak garden table, in the shade of a blue umbrella.

"He was very handsome, wasn't he?" she said, as she sat down in front of the glass of cloudy lemonade that Andrea had set out for her.

"Rory? Yes. He was."

"Did you know him…? I know you and Percy didn't get together until some years after he died."

"I did, actually. I taught him when he was in the sixth form. English. A long while before I'd even met Percy."

"What was he like?" Faith asked. "He has a look of – sensitivity. I should imagine he was very bright?"

"Oh yes." Andrea nodded. "He was an excellent student. He had a passion for literature. And he was extremely perceptive. Felt things very intensely – too intensely, perhaps. He had what you might call a 'romantic' temperament, I always felt. He wrote some wonderful poems. Several of them were published, in poetry magazines and journals. He was due to go up to Cambridge, but…" Andrea stared down at her glass, swilling the lemonade around and around.

"I'm so sorry," Faith said. "I shouldn't have brought it up. It must have been the most devastating thing, to lose him. Poor Percy."

"It was the worst thing that could have happened," Andrea said, slowly. "Percy was never the same afterwards. It broke him. And Sheila, too – Rory's mother. She had a stroke a few months afterwards, and then another, and the one after that killed her. It was remorseless, Faith, her decline. And I couldn't help thinking that the truth of it was, she died of a broken heart."

The sun had broken through the clouds now, and the Cartwrights's backyard was bathed in golden light. But somehow this didn't dispel the taint of sorrow that clung in the air. A cloying darkness that lingered in the house and around the backyard like a flock of black, brooding birds.

"It's good that we're leaving. This place has so many sad associations for Percy," Andrea said, as if she had picked up on Faith's thought. "Too many painful memories."

Faith nodded in agreement. She took a sip of her lemonade. It was very good – the sharpness of the lemons was blended with just enough sweetness, and there was a touch of elderflower, too. Andrea's skills in the kitchen were renowned in Little Worthy.

Against the far wall of the yard some metal sculptures stood. A couple of hares, leaping up to box one another with their front paws, and a leggy heron, staring down as if to pounce on a luckless fish.

"It's wonderful that Percy's managed to go on working," Faith said. "His sculptures have such life in them. Will he carry on with his metalwork when you're living in France?"

"I doubt it," Andrea said. "He hasn't made anything for a few months now, God bless him. He's got quite bad arthritis. It gets him in his hands, especially. They've been really troubling him the last few days. Terribly painful."

"I'm so sorry to hear that,' Faith said. Her watch was showing 12:20 now. It really was time that she took her leave and headed over to Cedars Lodge. "Thank you so much for this delicious lemonade. You must give me the recipe before you disappear to France."

Andrea promised that she would do so, and got up to show Faith out.

Cedars Lodge was a calm place. Well-run by kindly staff, Faith guessed it wasn't cheap to accommodate someone there. Though many of the residents were, as Ruth might put it, "not all there", Faith found their simple, steady routines a welcome break from the outside world. This wasn't a place where stories of murder would ever penetrate.

Moving among the patients, engaging in small talk, had an added dimension on this occasion, though. She'd always seen the old folk here as a different generation to her own mother, though some were probably of an approximately similar age. They might be suffering more advanced symptoms than Marianne, too, but this was the first time she realized they were on the same continuum. Would her mother end up somewhere like this, when caring for her became incompatible with Faith's busy life? There were worse outcomes, of course.

Back at the vestry, she began to tidy her remaining paperwork. At the bottom of the pile was the catalogue for the Sal Hinkley sale. Faith noted from the information on the cover that the auction was due to have started at 2:30 p.m. She flipped through the thick glossy pages, totting up the "reserve" prices that were listed – the minimum amounts that each painting would be sold for. The total came to around £300,000 – a staggering amount. She turned back to the page where the view of "St Francis's Church" (hopefully Patrick Mills would remember to change this, as he had promised) had been reproduced. The reserve was given as £20,000. *Would it make that? Or would it go for considerably more?* It seemed rather surreal that someone who didn't know St James's – someone who had probably never even heard of Little Worthy – might be willing to pay such a figure.

The sale would probably be over now. Commission made and the paintings going to their new homes. Would the money be heading to McGarran, after Mills took his commission? Faith still wasn't convinced by the mercenary motive.

She almost dropped the catalogue as the blood seemed to rush from her hands, leaving them cold. The pages splayed to reveal the strained, taut body of the young male nude she had seen hanging at Patrick Mills's gallery.

There was no mistaking it. Not the hair, the wild, intense young face. The burning eyes.

It was Rory Cartwright.

Faith checked the date of the painting. *Early 1980s.*

Sal Hinkley had known Rory – she had painted him. And not long before he died.

Everything seemed to have slowed down around Faith. Shock was weighing down her limbs, numbing her brain. But there was something she must do. Something she must clarify. She groped for her mobile phone.

"Peter? It's Faith."

"Hi!" Peter Gray sounded surprised to hear from her. "How're you doing? Great day, yesterday – I take my hat off to you, Faith, for setting all that up. We loved it, all of us. Me, Sandy and the kids."

"Thanks." Faith couldn't help it – her voice was slipping back into the clipped, economical tone of her days with the force. "Peter. I need your help."

"Well – sure. What is it?" He sounded a little wary.

"Oh, nothing much. It's just – I'm wondering if you could look up an old file for me."

"A *file?*" He was sounding really uneasy, now. "I'm not sure. Shouldn't we run it past Ben?"

"No," Faith said, quickly. "I don't think we should bother him with this. It might be nothing. It's just – I have a hunch. And I really need to check something out. Please, Peter?"

"Well, OK. Just this once. But don't make a habit of it."

Relief flooded through her. "Absolutely not, Peter. I promise. And – thanks!"

CHAPTER

18

The next morning, and Faith was back once more in the oh-so-familiar ambience of one of the interview rooms at police headquarters, breathing in stale, dry air and a faint tang of sweat and old trainers, despite that fact that from somewhere up above she could hear the constant, subliminal hum of the air conditioning. On the table in front of her lay a pile of photocopies that Peter had just made for her from a file in the archive room. She picked up the first sheet of paper, a witness statement, and read it once more.

> ... *I was driving back home to Ovington in my van, from a job the other side of Winchester. It was dark, but the moon was half full. There were no clouds in the sky. I was almost at Little Worthy, just coming round the sharp right bend about half a mile from the village, when I saw smoke rising up ahead of me. I slowed until I was going about twenty miles per hour as I came out of the bend. A Ford Fiesta had gone into a tree at the side of*

the road. The bonnet was all caved in and steam was coming up from the engine. The engine had been completely trashed. I think the Fiesta was maroon in colour – or maybe black. I didn't stop to look closely or take down the number plate, because I saw someone in the driver's seat. The driver's door was jammed shut, but I managed to get the passenger door open. It was a young man who'd been driving. He'd gone straight into the windscreen. There was blood all over his face. His nose was broken, and his forehead was split open. I recognized him as someone I knew from Little Worthy – Rory Cartwright. I wanted to get him out of the car but I didn't know if it was safe to do that, with his injuries. I picked up his hand, where it was resting on the gear stick, and it was cold. I couldn't feel a pulse. I was pretty sure he was dead.

Faith closed her eyes for a moment, picturing the scene. The moonlight shining through the shattered windscreen on Rory Cartwright's shattered face; his auburn hair stained even redder with blood.

"Are you done?" Peter stuck his head around the door, speaking in a low voice. "I've almost finished writing up my paperwork. I need to get going."

"Almost," Faith said. She was glad that Peter trusted her enough to give her privacy.

Since Faith was no longer a serving police officer, nor a relative of Rory Cartwright, it was rather a grey area as to whether she was allowed access to the information in the file. Peter was keen to get the photocopies back and shred them as soon as possible. It would be him in the firing line if there were any trouble.

"OK," he said. "I'll come back in ten. D'you want a coffee?"

"Please. Cappuccino? From the new machine?"

"Ah. You've got insider intelligence about the canteen revamp," Peter grinned and withdrew his head, closing the door behind him.

Faith carried on reading. Several statements by the officers who had attended the scene of the accident were appended to the witness statement. One of them read:

> ... I was called out to the scene of the accident just after 10 p.m. The driving conditions on the night in question were excellent. There was no water or ice on the surface of the road, and no oil slick present that might have caused the vehicle to skid into the tree. I couldn't identify any skid marks on the road, either.

A post-mortem report, also attached, revealed that the deceased had showed no trace of alcohol or drugs in his system. The verdict given at the inquest was "Death by Accident or Misadventure".

Her hands shaking slightly as she tried to take all this on board, Faith picked up the first witness statement once more.

> ... I left my van with the hazard lights on, and I ran to the nearest farm, which was a couple of fields away. I asked to use their phone to call 999. The ambulance came in ten minutes or so, and

*confirmed that Rory was dead. And then the police
came. As soon as I had told them everything, I got
back into the van and drove home.*

And there the statement ended. She'd read it three times now,
and each time she heard it in the voice of the witness himself.
For the name at the top of the statement, beside a signature,
was no stranger to her.

Gavin Wythenshaw

A few moments later, when Peter returned with his briefcase
and two take-out cups of coffee, she shared this information
with him.

"Would you look at that!" he said. "What does this mean,
Faith?"

Faith sipped the coffee. "Nothing," she said, with some
certainty. She'd had her own suspicions about Gavin, of
course, but in this case, she suspected she was looking at a pure
coincidence. The Wythenshaws had lived in Ovington before
they started the B&B down by the river. So Gavin would
probably have driven that road many times.

It was the car crash that interested her. A young man in
good health crashes head-on in dry conditions into a tree.

"Peter. I need your help."

"*Again*? What is it this time?" He cast an anxious glance
at the photocopies.

"Is there any way you could come on a visit with me?"

"To the Wythenshaws? We interviewed them already,
Faith. You know that." Peter's fair face was creased with doubt.

"No. Not to the Wythenshaws. There's something else

that's bugging me. I've got a hunch I know what happened on the night Sal died. I'll tell you all about it on the way."

"Right," Peter said, still looking doubtful. He scooped up the papers and stuffed them into the briefcase. "I'd better set fire to these first."

Faith's face must have betrayed her alarm. "Surely—"

Peter smiled. "Or I could use the shredder."

As he went to do so, Faith realized that Peter rarely told jokes. But his words set off another flash in Faith's brain. Fire – of course! By the second more pieces were falling into place.

It was Emily who came running to answer the door at the Johnston's house. She was wearing a pink tracksuit and a white plastic neck brace.

"Hello Emily. It's good to see you up and about already. That's wonderful," Faith said, her intense desire to cut to the chase mitigated a little by the sight of the girl's happy, smiling face. "How are you feeling?"

"Amazing," Emily replied, with a wide grin. "It's the first day of the summer holidays. Yaaay!"

"But what about this?" Faith pointed at the neck brace. "Doesn't your neck hurt?"

"Oh, it's nothing. Just a bit of whiplash, the doctor said. I can take it off next week. Thanks ever so much for coming to the hospital with me. Daddy was in such a state. I knew I was OK, but he kept fussing. I was really glad you were there to talk to him."

"You're very welcome," Faith said. "And I'm so pleased that you're feeling back on form."

"Me too. Diamond's been missing me," Emily said, with a grin. She was clearly completely unscathed by her fall. She plucked at the collar. "The doctors won't let me ride him at the moment, or even lead him out until this comes off. In case he knocks me over or something. *As if!* All they'll let me do is pat his nose over the stable door. But next week – whoopee – I'll be back to normal. I can't wait to take him out again."

"I'm pleased to hear that," Faith said, remembering Pat's words: *Horses can kill you, even when they don't mean to.* "But Emily – promise me you'll be very careful. Horses are powerful creatures."

"Oh, don't worry. The head riding instructor's going to give me some private lessons in the school, to help me sit on him properly – so I'll stay on if he leaps around again. Daddy insisted. And – when she thinks I'm good enough, she's going to teach the two of us to show jump!"

"Great stuff," Faith said, thinking that Emily must pose some serious challenges for Timothy and Clarisse's peace of mind.

"Hey – I know you. You're a policeman, aren't you?" Emily said, stepping round Faith and staring at Peter. "Why've you come?"

"We'd love to talk to your mum and dad, if that's possible," Faith explained. "Are they at home?"

"Sure!" Emily bounded off into the house. "Mum's here. And Dad. He's taken a couple of days off work, because of my accident. Follow me. *Dad!* It's Faith!"

Timothy and Clarisse were sitting in front of the television in the living room. Timothy jumped to his feet as soon as he saw Peter.

"Sergeant Gray! Look – I think there's been some kind of misunderstanding."

Peter gave him a sharp look. "What do you mean, Mr Johnston?"

Timothy held out both hands, palms upwards. His right hand was still bandaged, albeit with a slightly smaller dressing that the previous one. Peter stared at the dressing.

"You've hurt your hand. How did that happen?"

"Yes, yes. It's nothing. A rope burn, that's all."

Peter glanced at Faith, as if to say: *Did you know about this?*

"Look. I know why you're here," Timothy said, his voice rising a little. "It was an accident – OK?"

"What exactly do you mean by that?" Peter asked, his body tense.

Timothy continued, in a more measured tone: "What I'm saying is, we don't want to take things any further. We won't be pressing charges against the driver. Patrick Mills."

"Oh, right." Peter relaxed a little. "Are you sure about this? Your daughter could have been badly injured."

"Quite sure. Mr Mills was going a little too fast, but it was a blind corner. With those banks on the verge, and the hedge, there was no way he could see us. And the man was very shaken up – very contrite indeed. He's phoned several times since the accident to ask after Emily. It's our feeling, sergeant, that he's had a serious fright. He'll drive much more carefully in future. We don't want to take him to court."

"That's very generous of you," Faith said.

"Everything happens for a reason," Clarisse said, also getting up from her chair. It struck Faith, not for the first time, how elegant Emily's mother was. The flowered maxi-dress she was wearing would have looked rather frumpy on most women – but it clung to Clarisse's long limbs in a graceful, flowing line. She might just have stepped off a catwalk.

"Emily will be ultra cautious from now on when she's out on the roads. Won't you, my chick?" Clarisse said, brushing her daughter's cheek with a slim finger.

"Sure, Mum." Emily threw an arm around Clarisse's shoulders and gave her a gangly, affectionate hug. "I will."

"Actually, we didn't come to talk about Emily's accident," Faith said. "There's something I need to know – a very specific question I'd like to ask, if that's OK. About Eligius – or Diamond, if you prefer. But it has nothing to do with the accident."

"Fire away," Timothy said, looking puzzled. "We'll answer it, if we possibly can."

A vast red pantechnicon was parked up outside the forge, and a couple of stout men in leather aprons were loading a dining table into it. *We're only just in time,* Faith thought. *Another hour or so and the Cartwrights would have been on the road...*

She felt a sudden pressure as Ben gripped her arm. He'd come straight away and met them around the corner in his unmarked car. After a brief period of aggressive questioning towards Faith, and mutterings about loyalty in Peter's direction, he wore the expression of a man on a mission.

"You can't go in there alone."

"I have to, Ben," said Faith. "Trust me – this will be hard, but not because of any danger."

That terrible sadness she had felt, sitting in the backyard with Andrea. The vulnerability, the pain, so deeply buried under Percy's rugged exterior. Ben would have no conception of that. He would just march in and create havoc with no regard for anything but "the truth".

"Anything could kick off, Fay." His voice was low and insistent, but she could tell he was already weakening.

"I know these people, Ben. They're—" She couldn't say "parishioners" because that wasn't strictly true – "They're part of my community. I'll be fine."

She put her hand over his where it rested on her arm, felt the skin, slightly rough, and the strong knucklebones, their shape so familiar to her touch.

"Please, Ben. Don't worry."

His mouth twisted and he looked to Peter. "Let her, boss."

"Get on with it, then," he said, and pulled his hand away.

Faith stepped out of the sunlight and into the dark hallway, dodging around the aproned men, who were heading back into the dining room to collect the chairs. A tall, shadowy figure was stooping over the telephone table, scooping books and ornaments into a large crate. All the pictures and photographs were gone now, leaving pale, square ghosts of themselves against the yellowish distemper.

"Percy?" Faith's voice echoed off the bare walls. "Percy – I need to speak to you. Do you have a moment?"

Percy Cartwright was suddenly still, crouching over the little table, his huge blacksmith's hands gripping onto the sides of it. Andrea appeared in the kitchen doorway, a nervous, fluttering silhouette against the brightness of the open back door.

"What's going on? Percy? Are you all right? Is it your indigestion again?"

Percy shook his head. Slowly, as if his head and torso were so heavy that he could barely lift he straightened up and stared at Faith, his eyes sunk deep under the wrinkled lids.

"Yes," he whispered. "I have a moment."

Faith felt her body relaxing; lightness and warmth spreading through her limbs. *He knows why I'm here.*

"Percy, you've taken the picture down. The picture of Rory. Your son."

Slowly, the white head nodded, and the old man looked down at the crate that lay by his feet.

"It's Rory that I've come to talk about."

Percy was absolutely still again. Waiting for what she must say next.

"They knew each other. Didn't they?" said Faith.

"Who?" asked Andrea, frowning.

"Sal Hinkley and Rory," said Faith. "Why didn't you tell me, Percy?"

Percy did not move. It was Andrea who came running along the hall, a tea towel in her hand, to stand beside her husband. And after her, all the dark sadnesses of the house came rushing, too, like so many ragged, crazy birds.

The removal men had paused in their work, as if sensing the drop in temperature.

"Would you mind giving us some privacy?" said Faith. They duly edged past and into the hall to leave the house. Through the open front door, Faith could see Ben standing in the middle of the road, his arms folded.

"What's all this about, Faith?" Andrea's voice was hoarse with tension. "The estate agent will be bringing the buyers round to take possession in an hour. The sale's gone through, Faith. We have to give them the keys. *We have to leave.*"

Traces of mascara were smudged over the fine lines under Andrea's eyes, spoiling her usually immaculate presentation. She seemed to have aged ten years since yesterday, when the two of them had sat outside sipping lemonade in the sun. She turned to her husband, who was still standing motionless by the hall table. "Percy, darling? Will you explain to me what's going on?" She reached to stroke his white hair, but he made no response. It was as if he hadn't heard her urgent plea.

His face fixed on Faith. There was no anger in his eyes. They were devoid of emotion. His silence was profound. From a box somewhere, a clock chimed the hour.

"I'm sorry, Andrea," said Faith. "I know how stressful things are for you, with the move. But I have to ask Percy something."

Faith moved a step closer to the old man. "Why didn't you tell me about the connection between Rory and Sal, Percy? Why didn't you mention that they knew each other?"

Percy's body jerked, almost as if Faith had physically struck him.

"*Connection?*" Andrea gasped. "Don't be ridiculous, Faith. Rory would never have had anything to do with a woman like that. A *Bohemian* with no standards and no morals? How could there be a connection between them? It's the silliest thing I ever heard."

She was twisting the tea towel around her hands, pulling it tight.

Faith took a step closer to Percy. "You've packed the photo away. The photo of Rory."

Another tremor ran through the old man's body.

"Rory," he muttered. "Yes. Rory." He bent down and rummaged in the crate, pulling the framed photograph out from a cocoon of newspaper.

Faith took it from him and laid it on the table.

"He was very handsome, Percy."

The old man stared at his son's face, and a little moisture glinted in his deep-set eyes.

Slowly, with great care not to make any sudden movements, Faith took the Sal Hinkley sale catalogue from under her arm. She opened it at the page she had marked with a Post-it note, and laid it on the table beside the photograph. Percy Cartwright's eyes fixed on the pale body of his naked son. In the same instant, his body erupted in a violent convulsion of rage.

"What?" he shouted. "What is this?"

Andrea winced, ducking away from his raised voice.

"The whore!" he snarled, and his pale eyes blazed with hatred. "That's my son. And she—"

"Percy, no!" Andrea wailed. "Language, my darling." She turned to Faith, tugging at the dishcloth, binding it ever tighter round her fingers. "Will you please, please, just tell me what this is all about?"

Faith pointed to the two portraits on the table. The photograph and the sensual, vibrant oil painting.

Percy exploded again, sweeping both catalogue and photograph off the table and onto the floor with a savage gesture.

"Enough!" he shouted. "I'm not looking at this filth. I won't."

He pushed past them and staggered into the part-emptied dining room, where he collapsed onto one of the chairs and sat, bent double. Ben had rushed towards the door, but Faith met him and placed a hand on his chest. "Wait!" she said.

To her surprise, he did so. Faith peered into the dining room and saw Percy with his head in his hands. There were marks on those hands, Faith could see, now that he was in the sunlight. Bruises. Why hadn't she seen them before?

"You killed Sal, didn't you?" she said, softly.

The old man made no response, just sat with his bruised hands pressed to his face.

There was a movement at Faith's elbow. Peter had come into the hall now as well, and was standing just behind her.

"I'm so sorry about all this," Peter Gray said in a low voice, to Andrea.

Ben nudged Peter and raised a finger to his lips. "Let Fay handle it," she heard him whisper, and a rush of satisfaction ran through her veins. She stifled it quickly, and stepped into the dining room, slipping into the empty chair next to Percy.

"They had an affair, didn't they, Sal and your son?"

Percy's broad shoulders quaked. He dropped his hands and stared at her, his face a mask of desolation.

"My son. My only boy. She picked him up and used him and when she'd no use for him she screwed him up and threw him away. Just like that!" The old man raised his arm and flicked it, as if throwing something to smash against the wall. "He was a good boy, my son. A good boy with so much love in his heart. But she... she never had no thought but for herself. She used him, took what she wanted from him, and she walked away. And he—" Percy was convulsed suddenly, his chest caving in on itself, and then he continued, his voice a strangled whisper. "He wrote me a note to tell me why he killed himself. *I'm nothing without her. I'm nothing, Dad. I'm useless. I don't want to live any more.*"

Tears were running freely down over his wrinkled face in jagged tracks.

"My Rory," he said.

Andrea was weeping too. She dragged the tea towel across her face, spreading tears and mascara over her cheek.

"Percy. My dear, darling Percy," she sobbed. "You never told me. Why didn't you share it with me?"

Percy's eyes rested on his wife for a second, and then he

lifted his head, staring back into the past. "I thought she'd gone out of our lives for ever. Gone to the other side of the world. As good as dead to all of us back here in the village. I never thought she'd come back."

"But she did." Ben spoke softly, standing in the doorway.

"Oh yes." Percy's white head nodded emphatically. "She came back! I saw her every day, walking through the village, going up the hill to that hut to do her painting. Looking straight through me, like she didn't know who I was. What she'd done to me. To us. And I thought, *Leave it Percy. Leave it be.* But the day came I had to take the pony down to the riding stables. My wife's pony." His eyes glazed, and his breath was rasping in his throat.

"Eligius," Faith said, gently. "The model for the sculpture you gave to the church. Tell us about the reins, Percy."

Andrea made a confused wail, but Percy looked straight at Faith. Was that the flicker of a smile? "Very good, vicar," he said.

"Tell her!" said Ben, his voice suddenly harsh. He must have seen Percy's facial expression too – that note of triumph.

Percy nodded several times slowly. "I led him down to the stables that evening with all his tack on. And when I got there, I saw the buckle on the reins was broken. There's two of them, the reins, and each one fixes on to the bit at one end, and the other ends, they join up with a little buckle, to make one long rein. And it was broken, that little buckle."

Faith heard a slight grunt from Ben. He was itching to interrupt again, she could tell. He had no patience with all this seemingly irrelevant description. But Percy was a blacksmith. The Cartwrights had worked with horses for generations; the knowledge of the animals and all their equipment was in his blood. Such little details would be of great importance to him. And he mustn't be stopped – nothing must halt the flow of words that was pouring out from him.

"Well, I thought," Percy said, frowning, "I couldn't have some young girl – they're all youngsters, down at the stables – riding him with broken reins. I took them off the bridle and put them in my pocket to take them home. I was going to fix the buckle that night."

"That was very thoughtful of you, Percy," Faith said.

The old man seemed to be a little calmer. Letting him talk at such length was a good tactic. It was helping him to relax.

"So what happened then?"

"I saw her. Sal. Walking along past the Green, looking up at the sky with a little smile, like butter wouldn't melt. She was going to that hut of hers."

A shiver ran down Faith's spine. She'd seen that expression on Sal Hinkley's face a couple of times as she walked over the paddock past the church. An almost blissful expression, as if she were absorbing into herself the intense colours, the vibrant heat of the summer day.

Percy heaved a long sigh before continuing: "And I thought – no, that's not right. Her smiling like that. I can't let that pass. I must speak to her. Tell her what she did to my son, how she destroyed him. And his poor mother, too. She should know. If she knew, she wouldn't be walking round with that smile on her face."

Ben couldn't hold back any longer. He stepped forward, brushing past Faith.

"So what did you do then, Percy? Did you speak to her?"

"I waited a bit, to clear my head, because I was upset. And then I walked up round by Shoesmith's old place, and through the copse to the paddock. I knew she was at the hut because the door was open. I went over, and she was in there, fussing around with her paintbrushes. *Oh, hello Percy*, she says, cool as you like. *And what can I do for you?"* The old man's breath caught in his throat.

"What did you say to that, Percy?" Ben asked, his voice very steady, very neutral.

"I told her. *You could give me back my son*, I said. *My wife. You took them both away from me. I'd give anything, anything to have them back. Just for one hour.*"

Andrea buried her face in the tea towel. Faith wanted to go to her, comfort her, but Percy was still speaking.

"And she looked at me then, with those green eyes of hers. And she said, *Oh come on, Percy. Get over it. You can't hold me responsible for your son's mental health.* And I said, *He was in love with you. How could you leave him? How could you treat him like that?* And she just shrugged her shoulders. *I had to go, because of my work. It was a fling, Percy. He went into it with open eyes.*" Percy gave another long, rasping sigh. "I didn't understand what she meant at first. Work? What work? Piddling around painting pictures? That's not work. How could she put that before my son? I was standing there like a dead man, feeling nothing, trying to make sense of it all and then she screwed up the little rag she'd been cleaning the brushes with and she threw it away. Screwed it up and threw it away, like she did my Rory."

"Oh!" Andrea gave a little moan. "Oh, my poor darling. Please, that's enough. No more."

Percy might not have heard her. "That was it," he said. "That did for me. I couldn't stand by and see that. See her throw that rag away like she did my son. I had to put a stop to it." He collapsed forward again, elbows on his knees. All the breath seemed to have left his body.

"You used the reins, didn't you, to kill her?" Peter said, after a moment. "The reins from the pony's bridle. Where are they?"

"I think he must have burnt them, the morning after," Faith said. "The neighbours were complaining about a foul-smelling smoke. Pat told me. Leather stinks, when you burn it."

Percy's white head nodded, slowly. "Foul," he muttered. "Yes, foul, it was. But I had to get rid of them."

Ben moved to stand next to the old man, and put a hand on his shoulder. "When you're ready, sir," he said. "You'd better come with us. When you're ready."

Percy raised his head. His face looked a little brighter, as if washed clean of all the darkness that had dogged him for so many years.

"I knew I'd be caught, one day," he said. "I didn't care, not for myself. Only for her." He looked across at Andrea, who was staring at him with wide, horrified eyes. "I could've come and given myself up, if it wasn't for her. She wants us to get away, start afresh. T'would never work. I'm too old. This is my place, here. With my family." Percy Cartwright eased himself out of the chair and onto his feet. "I'm ready," he said, and stumbled out of the dining room after Ben, with Peter Gray following close behind. Faith was glad that Ben didn't read him his rights then and there. It would have been too much.

Andrea watched them go. It was very hot in the dining room, with the sun pouring in from the street outside, but she was shivering.

"What does he mean, his family? They're dead," she said, her voice thin and shaky. "All his family are dead."

As the adrenaline drained away, Faith was empty and numb. All she had left was the instinctive response to hold out her arms and go to Andrea.

"I'm here," she said, as moment by moment the fallout from the last few moments became clearer to her. The devastation that she had just dealt out upon Andrea, the woman she was now trying to comfort. "I'm so sorry. I'm here."

"What will I do?" Andrea gasped, her face against Faith's shoulder. "Whatever will I do, without him?"

Faith held her close through the waves of grief and pain. Outside in the street, Peter was helping Percy into the back of a police car, while Ben looked on. She waited for him to turn back and look for her, but he didn't. All his attention focused on Percy. Detective Shorter had got his man, the case was solved. And she, Faith, was no longer of any importance.

Another storm of weeping convulsed the woman in her arms.

After a time, Andrea lifted her head from Faith's shoulder, which was distinctly damp now, and gazed at her with red, bleary eyes. Faith gathered her courage. She must do something to try to mend the terrible damage she had wrought.

"Andrea. I'm sorry. If it could have been any other way…"

"Don't, Faith." Andrea's jaw was firm, now. "Don't apologize. It hurts so much that Percy lied to me all these years. One cannot live a lie." Her lip quivered again. "If he had told me the truth about Rory's death, I could have helped him. How could he ever heal, keeping it all inside like that, for all those years?"

Like a sword of light, the memory of Emilia Santa and her forgiveness towards her son's killers returned to Faith. *What good does it do in the world if I, too, am filled with hate?* But Emilia was one in a million. So many people had described Percy as "broken" by his son's death. Perhaps the wound of Rory's loss was just too great for him to recover from. Now the most important thing was to give Andrea the strength to move forward.

"He loved you. That's what you must hold on to, Andrea. Stay with that, through the coming days. Percy's going to need you very much indeed."

Faith drove away from the forge with a blinding headache. She'd stayed with Andrea for a couple of hours, taking on responsibility for fending off the estate agents until tomorrow, and also for contacting Andrea's sister, who came straight over from Southampton as soon as she heard the news. The Catholic priest from Andrea's church had promised to call by in the evening, too.

And now Faith was unable to focus on anything except the throbbing pain behind her eyes. She just about managed to drive over to the shop – going very slowly past the parked vehicles, as the headache was so intense she didn't quite trust her reactions to any oncoming traffic. Those inhabitants of Little Worthy who were campaigning for the speed limit to be lowered to twenty miles per hour would have been delighted at her cautious progress around the Green and up the narrow High Street. The shop didn't offer a great deal of choice in the way of fresh ingredients, but that was fine by Faith. She stocked up with some ready-made lasagnes and pasta bakes, and a selection of salads, plus some fruit juices and smoothies. Perhaps the headache was as much due to hunger and dehydration as it was to the stress of the day.

Back at the vicarage she unpacked the food in the kitchen, laying it all out on the long pine table, and then sat and looked at it. She didn't want to eat. She was empty, her body harbouring a deep sense of lack, but it wasn't food she craved. She made herself drink half of one of the smoothies and then had to stop and sit very still, weathering a storm of protest in her stomach at the sweet, acid juice. Too long since she had last eaten.

Alone at the table, as she was so many times every day, it was an automatic reflex to look up at the serene face of the Edwardian enamelled clock that she had inherited when she moved into the vicarage. *Five o'clock,* it told her. Just past teatime, a little while to go before supper. *I've spent more evenings in the company of that clock than any human being, this last year,* Faith thought. *I'm surprised I haven't started talking to it.*

Loneliness. Part of the human condition, to a greater or lesser extent. And Faith's modest share of it, right now, was nothing compared with what Andrea must be experiencing, now that she understood Percy's deception – how he had hidden his pain from her. And there would be more loneliness to come. Percy might receive some leniency when he came to trial due to his disturbed mental state, and the fact that the attack was not premeditated – but he would surely serve a long sentence. Andrea would probably spend the rest of her days alone. If she still went to Lourdes – and part of Faith hoped she did – then perhaps the influx of new guests on spiritual journeys of their own would provide some meagre solace.

And as for Percy – the loneliness he must have been enduring, existing for three decades in a self-imposed isolation, his terrible, corrosive sorrow keeping him apart even from Andrea – that was something Faith could barely contemplate.

Grief was such a complex emotion. One clung to the memory of the lost one. Faith did it herself. She still missed her father. She tried to remember his face, his voice, exactly as they were – yet she couldn't. The past fled her grasping touch. And there was so much of him she'd never known – like his relationship with Mum.

And was it the real, living Rory that Percy held in his heart for thirty years? *Of course not.* How could the memory that he clung to be absolutely accurate? Before his son died, the lad was moving away from him, starting to make his own choices. The memory of Rory was a construct, based on Percy's own needs, his own assumptions.

When it comes down to it, we are all alone, she thought.

Faith felt a sudden rush of warmth, and realized that wasn't quite true. She had something more absolute in her heart than shifting memories, and she offered a silent prayer of thanks.

Her phone vibrated, muffled in her pocket. She'd switched the ringer off while at Andrea's. Faith fished it out and answered without looking at the caller ID.

"Faith Morgan." Her voice felt dry and used-up.

"It's me." Ruth's familiar, slightly impatient tone. A tone that no doubt caused many of her colleagues at the council offices to quake in their shoes. Ruth hadn't risen to be the chief executive's PA by being cuddly and nice. Yet somehow, right now, Faith was very glad to hear it.

"Hello, you."

"Are you all right, Faith? You sound a bit weird."

"I'm just – knackered. Excuse the colloquialism, but I think the term pretty much sums it up."

"*Hmmm.* Knocked on the head, chopped up and put into cans for dog food? Is that it?"

"Exactly. It's been a hell of a day. What's up, Ruth?"

"I've got something to talk through with you, Faith. I'd

rather do it face to face, but I suppose the phone will do. If you've got a moment. If you're not too *knackered.*"

She cleared her throat. "Ruth – why don't you come over? You and Mum. I'd love to see you both. I was so busy when you were here on Sunday, too preoccupied to talk properly. Oh, and Brian, too, of course. If he'd like to."

A hasty afterthought, tagged on quickly – but Ruth's tone sounded a little warmer when she responded: "That's nice of you. But what about food? I could bring something from the freezer... I made a fish pie last week. A new recipe with salmon and prawns."

"No need," Faith said, smiling to herself. Most unusual, to be pre-armed like this, after her visit to the shop. "I've got everything in, don't worry."

After they had eaten supper, Marianne went out into the vicarage garden and found the watering can. Faith and Ruth watched her through the kitchen window as she walked up and down, sprinkling the desiccated borders with loving care. Brian had brought Ruth and Marianne over in his car – but after giving Faith a brief and totally unexpected hug – he had escaped to the pub. *I'll leave you ladies to enjoy some girl time...*

The conversation that Ruth had mentioned – *I've got something to talk through with you, Faith* – hadn't happened yet. No hurry, as far as Faith was concerned. It was so pleasant just sitting here in the kitchen, the scent of cut grass from the Green drifting in through the window. They hadn't even cleared away the table yet. Faith got up and made a half-hearted attempt to stack up some plates.

"Shall I save Brian some lasagne? It wasn't bad for pre-cooked, was it?"

"No need," said Ruth. "He'll grab a bite at the pub, I expect. You sounded awful earlier, when I rang. What's been going on?"

Faith explained about Percy's confession.

Ruth's eyebrows arched. "She had a nerve, then, coming back here. So cold. Leaving the boy in the first place was one thing, but just to turn up like that, almost on the father's doorstep – she sounds absolutely vile."

"I don't know."

"What d'you mean – *you don't know?* She rode roughshod over everyone's feelings, Faith. Bad, bad behaviour. If you ask me, she had it coming to her." Ruth tossed her head as if she had said the final word on the matter.

"I've felt like that, too. She wasn't an easy person. Very spiky. And yes – it was a terrible thing to leave Rory when he was so much in love with her. But she had to think of her work…"

Ruth snorted. "I'm sure you can relate to that one."

Faith flinched, inwardly. She knew what Ruth was implying – she'd never understood Faith leaving Ben.

"Well, I don't get it," Ruth said, with a sniff. "I think it was pure arrogance on her part to think she could come back here."

"Not entirely. She met up with her husband again…"

"Only so she could divorce him, I've heard."

"That's what most people assumed," said Faith. "Sal told her art dealer that she had divorced. She lied to him. She told her solicitor that McGarran wouldn't sign the papers. But I've spoken to McGarran since, and he says she never even mentioned divorce when they met. Why would *he* lie, now?"

"Why would *she* lie, before?" said Ruth.

Faith smiled. "Sergeant Gray told me this morning that they found the divorce papers in the recycling bin at the Wythenshaws's B&B. Sal must have thrown them there. The more I think about her, Ruth – the more I come to the conclusion that she came back to make amends."

"*Amends?* Honestly, Faith! After all this time? That's ridiculous."

Is it? Faith refrained from pointing out that Brian had walked out twenty years ago – and Ruth seemed to have no problem with *his* attempts to "make amends".

"Let me show you something," Faith said, walking across the room to fetch her laptop.

She opened it up on the table in front of her sister and loaded the scan of Sal's painting.

"Oh wow," Ruth said as the dramatic image of the church and the looming sky filled the screen. "That's stunning. Really powerful."

"It's Sal's painting. The one that should've been on the back cover of our booklet. But look, Roo…" Faith traced the slim shaft of vivid sunlight that broke through the clouds to strike a single grave in the churchyard. "That's Rory's headstone."

"Oh." Ruth's eyes were suddenly very bright. "Are you sure?"

"Yes. I had so much on my mind last week, I didn't put two and two together. But it's another attempt to make amends, I think."

Ruth nodded, for once at a loss for words.

It's as if Sal was making a pilgrimage of her own, she thought. *An attempt at atonement that led to her death.*

Marianne was calling from the back door. "Faith? I've reached the bottom of the water butt. What shall I do now?"

Ruth roused herself from her reflective mood. "There's rain forecast for later," she said. "I don't really know why Mother's bothering."

"Don't you remember what Dad used to say? That if you water first, it helps the rain to get down into the soil? Down to the roots of the plants?"

"Oh, yes!" A smile flickered over Ruth's face. "So he did."

Watering the garden had been the girls' responsibility. Sometimes, as a special treat, they were allowed to use the hose – though it was usually Faith who got drenched, rather than the thirsty plants.

Faith went to the door. "Come in and take some water from the tap, Mum. Unless you feel you've done enough. You've been out there for ages."

Marianne put down the watering can and slipped her fingers around Faith's wrist.

"There's lots still to do. Your poor flowers look like they've been fried," she said. "But I found these. They were growing in the lawn. Aren't they lovely? They used to be your favourites, when you were little." She held up a small bunch of daisies.

"Oh, Mum. They're sweet. Thank you." Faith stared at the tiny flowers. At their sunshine-yellow centres, and the tight frill of pink-tipped white petals. *How easy to lose the intense awareness of childhood – the pleasure in the simplest things that are right there under our noses every day.*

Looking into her mother's kind brown eyes, Faith suddenly remembered the conversation with her sister as the band played at the church. *I can't do it all on my own*, she'd said.

"Mum," Faith said.

"Yes darling?"

"Roo and I were talking, the other day, about your… situation. You know, how you live alone in Birmingham…?"

Marianne's eyes brightened. "Oh yes! I meant to tell you!"

"Tell me what?" asked Faith.

"Well, lovey. Brian took us out yesterday evening to look

at some very smart flats in Winchester. With a warden and everything. And I think, given the way things are, it would be a good idea if I upped sticks and came down here."

So that was the news Ruth had come to impart. Not quite what Faith had expected, but she felt a little weight lift from her chest. "But Mum – are you sure?" she said. "What will you do without your garden?"

"Oh, I'll just have to come and help you with yours," Marianne said. She leaned closer and patted Faith's arm. "You're not upset, are you? That I don't want to come and stay here, at the vicarage? We talked about it, last night, Brian and Ruth and I, about all the space that you've got, but I think I'll be happier with my own place."

"Whatever you want, whatever makes you happy – that's what matters."

Faith put her arms around Marianne. How was it that she hadn't noticed, on Thursday, that her mother had got smaller since Christmas? Faith could almost rest her chin on the top of her head.

"And I'm glad you're going to be closer to us, Mum," Faith said.

Now that she knew the vicarage would remain hers, its sanctuary and refuge undisturbed, she was surprised to feel not relief, but a sudden ache of loss.

Printed in Poland
by Amazon Fulfillment
Poland Sp. z o.o., Wrocław

60435327R00143